# Drustan
# The Wanderer

# Drustan
# The Wanderer

*A Novel Based on the Legend of*

*Tristan and Isolde*

Anna Taylor

*Saturday Review Press*

*New York*

Library of Congress Catalog Card Number: 70-186428
ISBN 0-8415-0165-3

*Saturday Review Press*
*230 Park Avenue, New York, New York 10017*

PRINTED IN THE UNITED STATES OF AMERICA

FOR *Jane Judge*

# Author's Note

The most familiar version of the story of Tristan and Yseult is probably that in Malory's *Morte Darthur*. In fact these legends grew up independent of the Arthurian cycle, though whether they were Breton, Cornish, or even Pictish in origin scholars do not agree. The derivation of Tristan's name – also spelt Tristram – suggests the last, and it is the Pictish original, Drustan, that I have used.

In my presentation of Drustan I have tried to avoid invoking Malory's Sir Tristram. I have worked from early sources of the legends, together with the considerable body of archaeological evidence available. My narrative draws on Malory at some points (notably the death of Arthur, and Drustan's involvement with Segward's wife) and I have succumbed to tradition in making Drustan King Arthur's contemporary. In fact, documentary evidence for Arthur's existence is very slight, and there are no contemporary written records for the period in which he is conjectured to have lived – the second half of the sixth century. The earliest is in the *Annales Cambriae* of A.D. 955.

I have substantiated my narrative with such historical facts as are established, picking out details of everyday life from among archaeologists' findings, and seeking for the thoughts and feelings of this extremely remote period in the nearest contemporary verse, that contained in the magnificent *Four Ancient Books of Wales* from which I have quoted part of the "Lament for Geraint Son or Erbin" on page 55.

I have followed tradition in situating Arthur's kingdom in Somerset and King Mark's in Cornwall. Kernow is ancient Cornwall, which comprises the under-kingdom of

Leones, where Drustan's father, King Cynmor, rules. (A sixth-century stone near Castle Dor bears the words DRUSTANS HIC IACIT CUNOMORI FILIUS – here lies Drustan son of Cynmor.) Castle Dor is a sixth-century hill fort near Fowey. Camlon is Malory's Camelot, the archaeologists' Cadbury Castle.

Ancient Wales was divided into three kingdoms: Gwynedd, North Wales; Powys, mid-Wales; and Dyfed, South Wales. Ynys Môn is the Roman Mona, the Isle of Anglesey. The River Hafren is the Severn.

Erin, or ancient Ireland, was divided into five constantly feuding kingdoms. Laighin is the modern Leinster.

Armorica is Brittany, whose people were Cymric – that is, Celts of the same tribes as those who settled in Britain.

The Dark Ages, though mostly undocumented, are a fascinating period. Sweeping changes occurred: waves of Saxon invasion, the decay of the remnants of Roman and Celtic culture, the coming of Christianity. I have tried to show in my characters the effect of these varying influences. Drustan is obstinately Celtic and pagan; Essylt is torn between her dark inheritance of witchcraft from her mother, and her father's Christianity; Mark tries to put Christian teachings into practice in a world still fundamentally pagan.

Essylt is the Old Celtic form of the name; Yseult the Norman, and Isolda the Latin. Brangwaine, Essylt's maid, and Gouvernail, Drustan's man, are found in Malory. Myrddin has of course inherited his name from his great forerunner, Merlin the Magician. Gwion was a Welsh bard, and Bedwyr is Malory's Sir Bedivere.

I wish to express my indebtedness to Hilaire Belloc's *Tristan and Iseult* and to Robert Graves for permission to quote the Song of Amergin from *The White Goddess*.

Finally, I must mention my gratitude to Michael Rose, whose tact and wit helped me to edit the present book from the 120,000 words my initial over-enthusiasm led me to write.

ANNA TAYLOR

viii

# Drustan
# The Wanderer

# One

The beginning, what's that? The coupling of father and mother, or her groans when, little more than a child herself, she gave birth to the child that killed her: me, Drustan, King Cynmor's first son. If that was the beginning then what shall I say about the time I don't remember, sucking an alien, indifferent breast, crying myself to sleep in my cradle with only the wind for a lullaby? Memories begin with walking, stumbling over the hard stone floors and tripping on the uneven edges, grubbing in the muck of the yard for treasure. Fear of abandonment, fear of my nurse's unkind fingers, fear of the dark.

The true beginning was the day my father married, as his second wife, the lady Cerridwen from the Islands of the Dead. Long ago, before the Romans came, ours had been a great kingdom. It had stretched from the place which is now called Land's End to these Islands, and the sea had once been rich fields where fat cattle grazed and men dug for tin and gold; but then there was the Inundation, the land was swallowed, leaving the kingdom of Leones only cliffs and high barren moors.

Beyond the Islands of the Dead lay rocks like giants' teeth, and stormy seas. No one dared sail too far in case he came to the edge of the world, where the ship would be caught by a great waterfall and swept over it as easily as the boats I made from leaves and sailed on the moorland streams. Great dragons and other monstrous beasts, their jaws always open, waited for ships, and swallowed them in one dreadful mouthful.

I hoped this fate might overtake the lady Cerridwen and her people.

Kanoel, my father's fortress, had been in a turmoil of preparation for her coming all spring, and now the day itself had arrived the women had been up since before dawn cleaning and cooking. Roasting joints of meat turned slowly on spits over the fire, there were piles of big round loaves and jugs of wine for the nobles. I was still hanging round the kitchens hoping to steal a mouthful, when I heard the soldiers down at the lookout blow their trumpets. All the maids gave joyful shrieks, dropped what they were doing and dashed out. I stopped only to grab a fat sausage and a fistful of bread, and ran after them, along the cliff path to the harbour.

Scrambling down the steps, I was thrilled by the sight of my father's guard assembled down at the quay. Cynmor himself towered above his troops. Dressed in a scarlet cloak, my father looked as handsome as a god. The people thronging the cliff path admired him, and talked excitedly, nudging each other to point out the sights.

The gaudy ship anchored in deep water, and sailors rowed the lady and her people ashore in small boats. The bright procession made its way gracefully across the harbour. Gulls screamed and the grey waves were whipped to foam by the winds.

My father welcomed the lady ashore. She was decked in fantastic jewellery which traders must have brought from the east long ages before, and a blue robe which left her white arms bare. Her cloak streamed from her shoulders like wings. On her brow a gold circlet set with stones flashed like fire in the sunlight, and her dark, curling hair fell in wide ringlets to her hips.

My father embraced her and led her up the cliff path to the fortress. The drawbridges were down and flowers strewed her way. Her people followed her, swarthy and brightly dressed, the hands of even the least of them heavy with rings. Behind came the people of Leones, gaping at the spectacle; myself last of all, dragging my feet and no longer hungry.

'What's the matter?' asked my friend Hywel, waiting for me.

I was thinking of my own mother who had bought my life with hers.

'I don't like the look of this woman,' I said.

'Keep out of her way then,' said Hywel. He envied me my freedom, for though I was only ten I had my own household, with Breisa, the servant, and Gorvenal, a battle-scarred veteran who taught me the use of arms.

'She'd better keep out of *my* way,' I said.

The ceremony had already begun, and we had to stand at the back of the hall. She had brought her own priest, who chanted in a high, uncanny voice, and scattered powder on the fire, which made it burn green and blue.

I could not see all they did, but after a long time the chanting ceased, and my father embraced his new wife and kissed her on the mouth. They clung together, her white arms hooked round his neck, while the people shouted approval. Men grabbed girls and kissed them too. The wedding ended in clamour and chaos. The guests fell upon the food and began to eat.

The lady sat beside my father and drank from his cup. She had odd slanted eyes, with blue paint on the lids. Everyone got drunk. When they had gorged themselves they started singing, quarrelling or making love. I looked for my father and the lady, but they had disappeared.

# Two

The lady Cerridwen bore my father three children in the years before I came of age: all sons, and with each one her hatred of me grew. I feared her instinctively, as animals fear, but my father stood between us, until the summer of my fourteenth year, when events forced him to go on campaign. Not events in Leones, but in neighbouring Lloegrys, where the famous King Arthur ruled. My father had served in Arthur's cavalry troop which had managed to halt the westward penetration of the Saxons. Since the battle of Badon hill there had been relative peace in the southwest; all the more shocking, therefore, was the news that came from Camlon, Arthur's fortress, early that summer.

My father told us calmly enough, but I could see by his eyes that he was angry. 'Rather hear it from me,' he said, 'than kitchen gossip.'

Arthur had been married for many years to Gwenhwyvaer, daughter of the king of Powys. Arthur had had no children by Gwenhwyvaer, though he had one son, Modred, by his own half sister. Modred was now of age, and it was he who had been the cause of the trouble. He had warned Arthur persistently that Gwenhwyvaer was the mistress of Lancelin, Arthur's second-in-command, and his best friend. At last Arthur could stand it no longer. He took his bodyguard, broke into Gwenhwyvaer's rooms at dead of night and found her in bed with Lancelin.

'It had been going on for years,' my father said. 'It was common knowledge, but Arthur chose to ignore it. He knew that any action would split his army in two.'

'And now?'

'Half of Arthur's men have gone with Lancelin. Arthur's

5

preparing an expedition to follow them to Gaul. Lancelin has lands somewhere in Armorica, but he's not of noble blood, just an upstart mercenary. It was Arthur who recognised his worth and encouraged him.'

'Why can't Arthur be content with his exile?' Hywel asked.

Cynmor shrugged. 'Perhaps Modred won't let him rest until Lancelin's dead. Perhaps it's his own pride. He's getting old. It can't have been easy all these years, knowing that he was cuckolded every night he slept apart from the queen.' Noticing Hywel's rather startled look he gave us each a push and told us to go and play.

'Father,' I said, hanging back, 'what will Modred do while Arthur's away?'

Our eyes met. Cynmor sighed. 'He won't be idle,' he said. 'Let's hope he's too much of a coward to do anything but scheme.'

'I hope so,' I said.

Before he left, in the great hall before all the nobles, my father formally proclaimed me his heir. It was like all our ceremonies, part Roman, only half understood, and part Cymric, only half remembered. I stood beside my tall father, conscious of his pride in his big body, his hawk nose, his thick black hair, and vowed that one day I would be as great a man as he. I looked with love on the people of Leones, and hoped that when I was king I would make it a great kingdom again, as in the days before the Flood.

Next day I watched him ride out at the head of his army. I would not believe that he might be struck down on some battlefield far from his country, or be brought home on a cart like other dead I had seen.

I took to sleeping in his rooms, not in his bed of course, for he had not given me permission, but on a pallet in a corner. Breisa the maid tried to tease me about it, but Gorvenal silenced her, reminding her that I was proclaimed now, and not to be mocked, that I could sleep where I liked. I dare say they were glad to be alone, for our quarters were cramped, and they had been growing self-conscious of late, punctuating their love-making with, 'Hush, remember the boy!'

My father's rooms were richly furnished, with a large carved bed, several ornate clothes chests, and brightly woven rugs on the floor; but they had an air of emptiness, the dank smell of unuse, now that all his followers had gone away. Even when Cynmor was at home, he slept in my stepmother's bed, repairing to his own rooms only after a quarrel or while she recovered from childbirth. There were a few of his belongings lying about, and that was as near as I could get to him in his absence.

I drew the hangings across the doorway and opened one of the clothes chests. A strong sweet smell rose to my nostrils from the perfumed wood. The chest had been brought by some traders in my grandfather's time. The slight smell of spice was always in Cynmor's tunics when he first put one on.

I tried on his tunics, and his cloak bordered with purple. Everything hung too loose on me, and ashamed, I took them off. In a second, smaller chest were linen undertunics, old cloaks, some brooches. The things filled me with sadness. I put them away. I had tried to make believe I was a king, but I was only a gangling boy. I went out into the practice yard, found Gorvenal, and wrestled with him grimly, trying to wear myself out.

A fortnight or so after my father's departure, one of the swarthy Island ladies brought me a message. I was covered with dust from scrapping with Hywel, and she had to wait while I picked myself up and wiped my sweaty face.

'The lady Cerridwen wishes to see you,' she said, avoiding my eyes.

I felt a sinking in the pit of my stomach. 'What for?' I asked.

She raised her eyebrows. 'It does not do to question the wishes of the queen,' she said. 'You are to come at once.' She walked away, swaying on the raised heels of her shoes.

'Well?' said Hywel. 'What's all that about?'

I wondered uneasily what wrong I could have done for

her to summon me like this, what punishment she might mete out. Or had she had some news of my father?

I went to wash my face. I was too proud to change my clothes, despite the sweat and grime. I was no child to be scolded, but my father's heir. She had no power over me. Hywel walked with me to the door of her rooms, and said, 'Good luck,' as if I was going for a thrashing.

I said, 'She'd better be careful, that's all,' and went into the hall feeling sick.

I had never been in the women's rooms before. She had had them painted and furnished like a palace. Thick hangings covered the walls, rugs lay edge to edge over the floor, and the air was heavy with scent. There were little tables with feet carved to resemble claws, chests bound with bronze and studded with knobbly gems, lamps made of clay and modelled to represent ships or strange beasts, and candlesticks with grotesque faces grinning the length of the shaft.

The maids kept me waiting in this ante-chamber before I was shown into her room. They stared at me and nudged one another, whispering together. At last, one came and announced that Cerridwen was ready to see me.

She sat smiling on a carved chair. She was wearing a rose-coloured dress and the new baby was feeding at her breast. Her long black hair flowed over her shoulders, over her white arms, almost to the floor. Her face was pale, for she had not been out of doors for some while, because of the baby.

Her two other children played with wooden animals on the floor and some kittens mewed in a basket by her feet. Her children were dark and sturdy, seeming identical but for size; both were dressed in red tunics.

'Come in,' she said, her voice very low. 'I'm glad you came. Your father's absence . . .' her voice trailed off. She gestured with one hand. 'This seems a good time for us to talk. After all, you are the heir . . .' She broke off again. I had lost my first sick fear, but I still felt uneasy. She seemed so strange. Perhaps the ordeal of childbirth, my father's departure soon afterwards . . . She sat very still, I

8

could not help gazing at her. She was the most beautiful creature I had ever seen.

'And they tell me you're the best fighter of all the boys,' she began in a brighter voice. 'The strongest and the swiftest. You take after your father, it seems.'

I blushed and wished that after all I had stopped to change my tunic.

'I admire him more than anything,' I said.

'And you've taken to sleeping in his rooms?'

Was this what the trouble was about? She didn't seem angry, but rather as if she was thinking of something else all the time.

'Yes,' I said. 'There are some books of his there . . .' Not that I could read them, any more than Cynmor could.

She raised her arched eyebrows. 'You're fond of books? I shall have some sent from home. They're being kept for my sons. Have you ever been to the Islands?'

'No, lady,' I said.

'The Islands are the most beautiful place on earth,' she said, 'far lovelier than this barren country; warmer and greener, with long golden beaches of firm sands and towering cliffs. In spring the flowers bloom there before anywhere else. In winter it never snows.'

'Why has a lovely place got such a terrible name?' I asked.

She fixed me with a gaze grown stern, her eyes narrowing. She said, 'Many years ago, before the Romans came, there was an earthquake and a flood, and the Islands were severed from the mainland.'

'I've heard tell of this,' I agreed.

'The Islands held fast to the Old Religion. Have you heard tell of that also?'

'No,' I said. I was ignorant of all religion, old or new.

'The Islands became a holy place. Dead kings and great nobles were taken over in boats and buried there. There are lines of burial mounds, grass-grown now and fertile. Flowers spring up on the graves in summer!'

I shivered. I couldn't bring myself to ask about the Old Religion. The baby in her arms had fallen asleep, his head

9

dark against her white breast. She rose, wrapped him tightly in his shawl and laid him down in his cradle in the corner. It was made of chased metal that shone; could it be silver?

The two little boys were playing quietly. They were the best behaved children I had ever seen. They did not shout or quarrel, yet they looked tough and quick-witted.

She came over to me, and taking my hand, led me across to the windows, shaded by blinds made of woven reeds. The sun shone brightly through them, making patterns of light and shadow on the floor. Here stood a table, thickly set with pewter dishes, bowls of fruit and cake.

'It's almost time,' she said. 'Will you eat with us?'

The table looked so delicate that I was afraid, but I nodded and thanked her. She rang a bell and two maids came in, one bearing a steaming tureen of broth and the other a large platter and a loaf of fine white bread.

The little boys were lifted on to their stools, the broth ladled out, and we began to eat.

As Cerridwen ate, a faint flush mounted into her cheeks, making her like a young girl. She seemed excited, beginning to talk, then breaking off, tossing her head and crumbling her bread between her long-nailed fingers. At last she sprang up, 'I know, Drustan!' she said, 'We must have wine! Wine to celebrate!'

I did not understand the cause of the celebration, so I kept silent. The broth was of chicken and very good. The children ate steadily, watching me with round black eyes over the rims of their bowls.

Cerridwen returned with two wine cups, made of gold and thickly embossed. She stood before me, hesitating a moment. I thought she intended me to rise, so I did so. Her eyes looked wild and her hands shook so that the wine swirled in the cups. I was as tall as she. I thought, why is she trembling? Why has she asked me here? Can it be that she loves me?

She put the cup down firmly in my place and sat down opposite me. I was trembling too and my face was hot. Her fingers gripping the stem of her cup looked very white.

10

'A pledge!' she said, raising her cup. 'We'll drink to Leones: Cynmor's kingdom.'

At this the children, so good and silent till now, began to clamour to be allowed to drink as well. 'Hush!' said Cerridwen sharply. 'I'll fetch you some raspberry syrup by and by.' She took a long draught from her cup.

I made as if to follow, but the stuff smelled so pungent that it turned my stomach.

'Come, then,' said Cerridwen impatiently. 'Pledge me!'

I gazed at her curiously. All colour had drained from her face, except for two bright spots burning her cheekbones. I took a mouthful of wine; my stomach heaved, and I spat it half across the table. Some dribbled on my chin and stung and burned among the down of my first beard.

She had risen to her feet. Her breasts heaved beneath her dress. The baby in his cradle began a low monotonous wail, and the children slid from their stools and sidled round the table. Her eyes, holding mine, were kindled with hatred. And I'd thought it was love. Suddenly she screamed, 'No! Don't touch it!' Her eldest son had seized my cup in his fist and made as if to drink the dregs that were left. He let out a howl and dropped the cup. The lees of wine and poison spilled, staining the fine rug underneath the table.

I said, 'Why? I've never hurt you.'

She said quite coldly, 'You stand in the way.'

'I am my father's first son,' I said. 'It's just that I should inherit —'

She gave a gasp of laughter. 'You? *You*'ll never be king. I know the future. You will wander the earth. You will never be king in Leones.'

'Why then try to poison me?'

'To do you a kindness,' she said.

Breaking into my solitude, into my lonely reveries of fear and foreboding, came a messenger from my father. The expedition had been bloodless, not a man lost. Arthur and his men had laid seige to the town where Lancelin took refuge, but almost immediately Lancelin had surrendered.

11

He and Arthur fell on each other's necks and peace was declared. Cynmor bade me come to Castle Dor to meet him.

Castle Dor was the stronghold of Mark, who was king of all Kernow; Leones was his subject-kingdom. King Mark was also my uncle, my mother's brother, and this involved him in special obligations to me. Mark had not chosen to remember his duty to me before, but taking the opportunity afforded by their soldiering together, my father must have reminded him that I was almost of age.

Gorvenal rode with me, and Hywel too, excited at the adventure. It was the first time I'd ever left Leones, and as we rode further and further from Kanoel my spirits lifted for the first time in many weeks, and it almost seemed as if my stepmother's awful warning had never been uttered. When the summons arrived, I had vowed to myself that I would tell Cynmor that she had tried to poison me, but as we rode over the rutted road in the sharp summer sunlight, I knew that I never could. It was part of the warning, a dark thing that would stand forever silent between her and me.

# Three

Castle Dor, the great hill fort, was thronged with people. The army was not long returned, and though Arthur had gone back to Lloegrys, Mark's allies had not yet dispersed. Cheated of booty by the unexpected truce, they were determined to enjoy what they could in the way of feasting and entertainments before going home. It was harvest time, too, and there were motley bands of reapers, toddlers and grandmothers, young women carrying their babies on their backs, while children played among the stubble. Most of the men lounged about in the yard, talking or playing dice.

I was scanning the crowds for my father when I noticed two odd-looking figures; a couple of men, one naked but for a ragged strip of cloth round his hips, the other swathed in a long thick brown robe. The naked one was very thin, his bones showed like the ribs of a leaf. The front part of both their heads was shaved, behind the hair hung to their shoulders, matted and filthy. I stared at them.

'Who are they?' I asked Gorvenal.

'Christians,' said Gorvenal, 'a new religious brotherhood. They've made many converts in Lloegrys. Don't let your mouth hang open like that, Drustan,' he went on, digging me in the chest with his sharp elbow. 'It isn't becoming in the heir to a kingdom.'

That evening we went with my father to the king's hall. I had thought that we were splendid at Kanoel, but now I saw we were barbarians beside the nobles of Castle Dor. In the huge hall, brightly lit with three-branched candlesticks, King Mark sat at a high table, and facing him, along benches which filled the building, sat the flower of Kernow, the captains and troops that Arthur had led into Gaul. They were laughing and drinking, still discussing the expedition. It seemed that no one who had been across to Armorica could talk about anything else.

We walked up the gangway, my father in the centre with his arm round my shoulders, Hywel slightly behind. Mark stood up and saluted us.

The bright lights tinged his fair hair and curly beard with red, and flamed in the golden collar he wore round his neck. He was a handsome man, not tall, but broad and well-made, with a noble face and a winning smile.

'Cynmor! So your son has come at last. I couldn't mistake him, he's the image of you.' He embraced first my father and then me. 'Drustan? Isn't that your name? I've wanted to meet my sister's son for so long, and your father has nothing but praise for you.'

I shivered at the remembrance of what *she* had said: *you will wander the earth.* I felt ready to worship Mark for his kindness. I couldn't speak.

My father presented Hywel, and King Mark smiled at him. 'You're especially fortunate to have come tonight. I have asked the bard to entertain us.' Then he turned to a slave standing by and said, 'Send for him.'

After more fair words, we went to our seats and ate and drank our fill. And then the bard came in.

He walked gracefully down the centre aisle of the hall, between the tables, acknowledging the cheers and hand-claps with a slight motion of his head, which made his long fair hair ripple like a cornfield. Poised, taut, slender; these were the epithets that came to me later, when I had been taught the use of words, but at the time when I saw him first, I thought simply, it's magic. He moves like a dancer. He knows some mystery. And I felt afraid.

He carried an instrument in his right hand, a tall delicate harp, strung with more strings than I could count. The polished wood was unlike any wood I knew. The man, too, did not behave like any entertainer I had ever seen. Jugglers had sometimes wandered as far as Kanoel, and once a troop of players who had lost their way, but they

14

were ingratiating and subservient. This bard was like a noble. He was richly dressed and wore many jewels. He bowed to King Mark, but as a sign of respect, not fear.

'Greetings, lord,' he said. 'Which of my countless stories and songs will please you tonight?'

Mark smiled at him a little quizzically and thought a moment. Then he said, 'There's a lad here who's never heard a poet before. What about the "Song of the Battle of Badon"? It tells how Arthur defeated the Saxons. Do you know it?'

The bard raised his eyebrows. 'Of course.'

'Good!' cried Mark loudly. 'We shall hear it at once!' He had started to slur his words. He was getting drunk. The girl at his side laughed aloud and tugged his girdle for attention. He bent down to her and she started whispering in his ear. I wondered at seeing him lose his dignity.

The bard paused for quiet, and when the whole hall was still he began to play the harp. He plucked the strings singly with his nails in a swift headlong succession of vibrating notes, and the melody rose and fell like the waves of the restless sea round Kanoel. When the music was done he began to recite, punctuating the words with more music, and playing between each verse.

When he ended with a final triumphant flourish on the harp, there was a moment's silence, and then the hall was filled with applause, men clapping their hands and banging their cups on the table. Of course it was a subject that couldn't fail to please. The bard bowed once and remained upright. Mark beckoned him over, and pulling a bracelet off his arm, gave it to him. It was gold and looked heavy. The bard slipped it over his wrist with a nod of thanks.

When the applause had died he began a second song that Mark requested, the 'Tale of Suibne and Éorann'. It was plaintive and touching. Mark and his girl began to exchange kisses. I felt myself growing red. When the thing was ended, under cover of the clapping I whispered to Hywel, 'I'm going. I've had enough.'

He looked surprised, but nodded and followed me outside. I noticed that my father's place was empty. He must have left before us unnoticed. I knew that he did not care for music or poetry.

I sat down on the porch and Hywel sat beside me. He was my best friend but that evening I was full of conflicting emotions and wanted to be left alone. After the sweltering heat engendered by so many bodies crowded together in the hall, the fresh air felt cool and sweet. It was a beautiful night with a bright moon half full in the clear sky. The yard was empty and quiet, but for the footsteps of sentries on the wall walk and the sounds from the hall where the bard had begun another song.

Hywel sensed my mood and after a couple of attempts at conversation he said he would go to bed, pressed my arm, and left me.

I sat for a long while, hunched in the shadows, crying in the only way that I thought fitting then, behind my eyes. I didn't understand what was troubling me. My heart ached with the beauty of the night and the bard's music. Then I looked up and found him standing over me. He seemed to have been conjured up out of the night by my thoughts.

He smiled at me without speaking and turned to go.

'No,' I said. 'Stay, please. I've never heard a poet before. I only came to Castle Dor today.'

'What is your name?' His ordinary speaking voice was lighter than the one he used for reciting, and rather colourless. He sounded hoarse too, for they had kept him at it for ages asking for song after song.

'Drustan,' I said. 'I'm heir to Cynmor, king of Leones.'

'I saw you listening. I'm glad you enjoyed yourself. Perhaps you could prevail upon your father, who I know isn't overfond of poetry to invite me to Kanoel.'

'I'll try,' I said, and as he made again to turn away, 'Were you really there, at the battle of Badon?'

He tried politely to hide his laughter, but it got the better of him. He sat down beside me on the wall. 'I was still a baby when they fought that battle. I learned that song from the bard who made it. He was there.' He must have sensed my longing, for he asked gently, 'What is it?'

16

'Would you teach me?' I asked. 'Could you teach me, to play the harp and make up poems like those?'

He mocked me delicately. 'You're like a child with a new toy. Tomorrow something else will have caught your fancy.'

'No,' I said, 'No, you don't know.' Her words had come back. *You'll never be king.*

His eyes narrowed as he watched me, almost knowing my thought. 'You're a king's son. How could you go to the College on Môn? How could you give up seven years to the study of druidic lore?'

'I don't know...' I felt suddenly very sleepy and childish. It was midnight and I had crammed as much adult experience as I was capable of into the day.

'Come along,' said the bard. 'Do you know where you're supposed to be sleeping?'

Half led by him I found the king's hall. Gorvenal was playing dice outside and cursed me loudly for making him wait up. In the end I never said goodnight, or even thought to ask the bard his name.

Though I was so tired I couldn't sleep. I tried to piece together the words of the bard's songs, but being untrained I failed utterly. Then I thought about Cerridwen, and fear filled me. What was it in my future so terrible that she considered it kindness to poison me? Or had it all been a sea witch's lies? One thing became clear to me as I lay there sweating in the dark, that I must not go back to Kanoel, for if I did she would find some way to destroy me. I must go away, I must acquire knowledge, so that my strength could equal hers, and then I would go back and challenge her.

My only hope lay in the bard. He has the key to knowledge, I thought. The druids have it. I will make him take me to Ynys Môn. Then I felt calmer and quite happy, and relaxed into vivid dream. The bard and I were riding on horseback across a flat plain through an avenue of trees. He was playing the harp and I was singing. The trees bent over until their leaves swept the ground.

17

# Four

I sought him out as soon as I woke the next day. He was at breakfast in the great hall, his head bent over a bowl of broth. I stood for a moment watching him and approached shyly, but he smiled when he saw me, and motioned me to sit down. I sat and drank some ale.

'You're as lazy as I am,' he said. 'Everyone else has finished and gone long ago.'

'I couldn't sleep,' I said. 'I was trying to remember one of your songs.' I bit into an apple. 'It's a beautiful day. Will you walk a little way with me?'

He said, 'That's the most sensible suggestion anyone's made since I arrived here. Which way is it to be? Up the valley or towards the sea?'

'The sea,' I said. At Kanoel there is always the sound of the sea, and already I felt caged within this fortress where so many people lived close together that it was impossible to get away by oneself. We wandered down through the village. 'How many soldiers there are!' I said. 'Whose are they and why do they stay here?'

'Maybe the gods know,' he said, 'I don't. I hope you haven't dragged me off to talk about politics. Politics bore me.'

'No,' I said, rather regretfully, for I had never had the chance to be bored by anything so sophisticated.

We took a short cut across a field that the reapers had cut. The stubble hurt my bare feet, so I ran on ahead to get it over quickly. I waited for him by the hedge.

'What is your name?' I asked.

'Myrddin,' he said, 'after Myrddin the druid.'

I had heard tell of him. 'Myrddin the magician?' This was how he had figured in the tales which Breisa sometimes told me.

'So some call him,' said Myrddin.

We had come out on to the bank of the river. We paused for a while to watch the broad stream which looked like glass in the sunshine. Though the water was low, it was fast running.

'Let's go and see the ships downstream,' I said.

We walked along the path by the river, Myrddin in front, me following behind. Trees dappled us with light and shade. We didn't talk. The river grew broader. We saw a merchant ship with bright sails.

'I wonder where that comes from,' I said, pointing.

'Armorica, by the look of her,' Myrddin said. 'One of the wine carriers.'

A little way from the river mouth there was an island in midstream. It was small and sandy, with a heap of rocks in the centre and a gnarled old tree. It seemed to me somehow sinister; and I shivered in the sunshine.

Standing on the headland, we watched the sea. I took deep breaths of salt air.

'I feel alive again,' I said. 'I don't know how all those people can bear living at Castle Dor.'

He laughed. 'Wait till you've seen a town.'

He lay face downwards on the grass, and I sat beside him.

'You must think I'm very ignorant of the world,' I said.

'Perhaps it's good to be ignorant of the world.'

I was impatient with abstractions. I said, 'Tell me something I don't know. Tell me about the first Myrddin, the magician.'

'The druid,' said Myrddin. 'He was the first of the great poets; a philosopher, a magician and a bard. He set up seven Colleges among the Cymry, schools of druidic initiation. The most important was on the island of Môn, but when the Romans conquered us, they persecuted the druids, sacked Môn and slaughtered the people. The Romans have gone, but they did their work too well. What have we left? Some poetic lore, a little magic, less philosophy.' He had forgotten me, he was talking for himself. 'It's like trying to read in the dark. Impossible! Is it a wonder I'm put at the common table, and have to take *payment*, a bracelet warm from the king's arm, slipped on to mine at the end of a song as if he were paying a *whore*!'

I could hardly console him, for I was still a boy, an ignorant child beside a learned man. I sat until he grew still, listening to the waves, and then I said. 'Was it different once?'

'Different?' His tone surprised me. It was light and unconcerned, as if the passionate outburst had never been. 'Oh, yes, very different. Before the Romans came a poet was the equal of a king. Indeed, he was the master; a bard could make and unmake a king. Kings paid us reverence. As one of the Triads says:

> It is death to mock a poet,
> death to love a poet,
> and death to be a poet.'

For the second time Myrddin had made me afraid. I was on the point of turning, going back to Castle Dor, giving up my plan, but suddenly he smiled at me, and my foreboding melted like ice in the mouth.

'By all the gods!' he cried, 'I must be in low spirits. Whatever possessed me to bore you with all that stuff? It's past now. Nothing *I* can say will change it. Why try? Why not enjoy what we have?'

He swept his hand through a half circle, indicating the grass beneath us, starred with daisies, the radiant sky, the ocean.

'I shall be glad to go home,' he said. 'I'm weary of travelling.'

'Where is your home?'

'Degannwy, the fortress of King Maelgwn of Gwynedd. It's near to the bardic college of Môn, and my wife —'

'You're married?'

He smiled. 'Yes, and I've a daughter, born last year.'

I had gathered a handful of daisies, intending to make a garland, but instead I found I had crushed them in my fist. Myrddin said, 'Drustan, we must start back.'

I knew that if I didn't speak now, I never would. I said, 'Will you take me with you?'

'*What?*'

'When you go north. Will you take me with you?'

'But you belong here. You're King Cynmor's heir, aren't you? Why do you want —?'

'That's my business,' I said. 'Just tell me: will you take me, and help me to enrol at the bardic College on Môn . . .?' My tongue stumbled on the unfamiliar name. 'I want to be a poet.'

Myrddin looked at me very hard for a long time. 'How old are you?'

'Fourteen.'

'Can you play any instrument?'

'No.'

'Can you read Latin, do you know any other tongues, any Mathematics?'

'No.'

'Look at me.'

I gazed, and at first I saw only his eyes, grey, with darkening irises, fringed with long fair lashes, but then I seemed to stare through his eyes. The grey became troubled, stormy. I could hear the wind.

'Tell me what you see.'

'The sea. I can see the sea, but it's winter, the sky's stormy.'

'What else?'

'I can see a beach, with cliffs beyond, and, yes, there are men descending the cliffs, coming towards me across the beach.'

'Describe them.'

'They wear long grey robes, their faces are hidden. They're coming nearer. There's some kind of chanting, or perhaps it's the noise of the wind. The first is near me now. I can see below his hood. His eyes. Myrddin, Myrddin, they're *my* eyes! I am looking at myself.'

'It is enough for now,' he said, and the eyes into which I stared changed colour, were once more grey, and friendly. I could feel the sun.

Myrddin drew a long breath. I grabbed his hand. 'What happened? What did you do?'

'It's nothing,' he said, in a light, tired voice. 'It seems I shall be taking you with me . . . What will your father say?'

'Leave me to worry about that,' I said.

Now that the matter was settled, we walked back to Castle Dor in silence.

'Where've you been?' Hywel asked. 'Cynmor has been looking for you all the morning.'

'I got up late and went for a walk,' I said. 'Do you know where he is? I'd better go and apologise.'

'I believe he's gone to the cock-fight. I'll walk over to the pit with you if you like.'

My father and King Mark were among the excited ring of spectators. I arrived too late to be very interested for the fight was almost finished. A big black cockerel was engaged in pecking a smaller red one to death, hindered only now and again by a lucky slash from the spurs on the dying bird's feet. A cheer told me it was over. I shouldered through the dispersing crowd to my father.

'I thought for a while Copper had him,' King Mark was saying, trying to tug off a ring that had stuck on the joint of his first finger.

'Black Slasher had the weight and the size,' said my father. He grinned. 'It always tells in the end.' He put his arm round my shoulders and ruffled my hair. 'Doesn't it, Drustan?' Then he remembered his anger and shouted, 'Where have you been?' just above my ear.

I blenched and Mark, laughing, went away. Hywel must have drifted off; he never did like cock-fighting.

'Well?' Cynmor said.

'I went for a walk.'

'Alone?'

'With Myrddin the bard.'

'That effeminate wastrel! I was looking for you to ask if you want to stay for the boar hunt Mark's planning. If you do, we'll wait. Otherwise we'll go home tomorrow.'

There is no forest in Leones big enough for the wild boar to live. This hunt in the great Moresk forest would have been my first chance and I was touched that Cynmor had remembered. I looked up at him, at the hawk-like nose, the thick eyebrows. His hard, lined face was not softened by the merrymaking at Castle Dor. I resolved to be as strong as he.

'Father, I must talk to you.'

'Come and have a drink.'

There was so much noise in the hall that we had a kind of privacy. 'Well?'

I began. Most of it was unplanned, but I found the words rolling off my tongue most satisfactorily. 'Father, you know that I'm proud to be made your heir, that I love Kanoel and the land of Leones more than anything, except perhaps you – '

'Get on with it,' he said, and drank his ale.

'It's because of this that I feel I'm not ready to rule yet.'

'Damn it, boy!' he exploded. 'Nobody's going to ask you to for another fifty years.'

'Listen,' I said, 'I can't read, I can't write. I'm ignorant, father.'

'No more can I *read* or *write*,' he said gruffly. 'It's never stood in my way. You've a head on your shoulders and a strong right arm, haven't you? What more do you want?'

'I want to go to Ynys Môn.'

'Where in hell is that?'

'Off the coast of Gwynedd. There's a druid college there.' I was careful not to use the word *bard*, which I knew would enrage him.

'Damn it, Drustan!' he shouted. 'Who's been putting this wild scheme into your head? I won't let you go away. I want you to come with me on my next campaign. The gods know we've had little enough to do with each other all these years, since your mother . . .'

We stared at each other across the table, he flushed with rage, I pale and deadly calm.

'You can't forgive me,' I said, 'because of my mother . . .'

'That's not true,' he said. 'Be careful, boy, or I'll thrash you until you can't stand.'

The hall was quiet now. Everyone was listening to us.

'I am my own master,' I said, and Cynmor tossed his ale full in my face.

Gasping and spluttering, I wiped my wet hair out of my eyes and saw that King Mark had come over to us. He stood by my father, his handsome face full of concern.

'What's this?' he said. 'If a father and son quarrel who can be sure of his friends? Sit down all of you,' he gestured to the gaping throng, 'and bring some wine for me and my kinsmen here. Now, what's the matter?'

I dried my face on the hem of my tunic and said nothing. A slave brought the wine and we drank in silence. At last my father said, 'This brat here,' he indicated me with an oblique gesture, not turning his head in my direction, 'has decided to acquire an education. Rather than come back to Kanoel with me, he wants to go off to Gwynedd for the gods know how long, until he feels ready to be a king. As if I intend to die yet!' He glared at me chillingly and looked away. I sat still and felt the ale dripping down the back of my tunic.

'You know,' said Mark after a pause, 'that doesn't sound such a bad idea to me. Of course you're hurt that he won't be going home with you, but in these days a man should try to gain all the learning he can. Perhaps when you come back you'll be able to teach me a thing or two, eh, Drustan?'

A light-hearted speech; but I knew, and Cynmor knew, that it meant I should go to Môn. Mark was my father's lord, and if Mark was my ally, then he was the only one I needed. I gave him a brief glance of thanks. I dared not speak for what it would do to my father.

Cynmor drained his cup slowly. At last he said, 'Very well. But remember: if you go, you go without my blessing.' Then he threw down the cup and strode out of the hall.

I took my leave of King Mark and almost wept. 'Give me your blessing, lord,' I begged, for my father had withheld his.

'I'll bless you gladly, Drustan,' Mark said, 'if you tell me in whose name to do it. Which god do you follow?'

'No god I can name,' I said.

So instead of a blessing he kissed me.

# *Five*

We rode north from Castle Dor, following the track that runs alongside the river, till we struck the road that meets it, west to east, a little way from the source. We kept to this road across the barren upland moors, skirting the high ground to keep the horses fresh, and made camp when evening came. Next day we made even better headway; these roads were in good repair.

'This is King Arthur's territory,' said Gorvenal. 'His fortress is over there, at Camlon.' He pointed to the south. 'If I had my way that's where I'd be taking you, Drustan.'

Myrddin, who had objected to Gorvenal accompanying us from the first, smiled briefly. 'Don't let me stand in your way,' he said.

For a moment I was tempted. I reined in my horse and sat listening to the song of the birds in the thick wood that flanked the road. Gorvenal rode on in a huff, but Myrddin turned his mount round and came back to me.

'With any luck we'll be at the coast tonight,' he said. 'By this time tomorrow we'll be in Powys.'

'Have you been to Camlon?' I asked him. He nodded. 'And what is it like?'

'Like King Mark's fortress, like any of them. These soldiers are all the same. They love power, nothing else. Oh, it's true, Arthur is generous, Arthur is brave. Arthur leads his cavalry into battle, and when he's not killing spends his time in the Christian sanctuary on Ynys Witrin praying for his soul. But what he wants —'

'Is *he* a Christian?' I asked, remembering the hermits I'd seen at Castle Dor.

Myrddin nodded, not to be diverted from his theme.

27

'But what he *wants* is power. If he could drive the Saxons into the sea he would be king in the south.'

'Surely —' I began.

Myrddin held up his hands for silence. 'How quiet it is!' he said. 'Listen to the birds.'

I looked at him, his withdrawn face, the fine profile half hidden by the mass of his hair.

'Do you *want* me to come with you?' I asked.

'Do you doubt it, Drustan?' he said.

I didn't answer. I knew I had forced myself on him, and now that my father and my home were so far behind I was feeling as lost as a child whose mother's skirt is plucked from its desperate little hand in the midst of a crowd.

'Come,' he said smiling. 'We must catch Gorvenal. It's dangerous to separate.'

And he was off like the wind, leaving me startled, and somehow disappointed, to follow as quickly as I could.

That night we slept on the floor of the back room of a baker's shop at Aquae Sulis. We arrived in the city late at night and had been unable to find lodgings anywhere else. The ancient city was crowded with travellers who had come to drink the medicinal waters and take hot baths to cure their aches and pains. Soldiers came in hope of curing poisoned wounds; but the people who filled the city to over-flowing were refugees. Some had travelled from the Saxon-occupied lands in the east, others had come from as far away as Erin or Armorica. Most were on their way somewhere else, searching for a settled home free from fear of invasion. Thus much the baker told us, wiping his floury hands on his apron, 'But these are unsettled times. We must just do what we can.' He went back to kneading his dough, glancing uneasily round his warm comfortable shop. Trade was obviously booming for him. He and his family were working all hours to make enough bread to meet the demand, and we had to dig deep to find the price he asked for a few hours' sleep on his floor. But he knew that if the barbarians did make war again his wealth would be no use to him, lying with his throat cut on a split bag of flour, nor to his wife or pretty daughters, raped and carried off as slaves.

'Do you think the Saxons will come again?' I asked Myrddin as we unpacked our saddle-bags and tried to beat the flour dust out of the extra blankets the baker lent us.

'Of course they'll come back,' said Myrddin. 'They're defeated now, it's true, but how long do you thing it'll take them to recover? Ten years, twenty years? A generation is what I'd bet. And then what's to stop them taking all they want?'

'King Arthur?'

'Do you think Arthur is immortal? That would be our only hope . . . Now sleep Drustan. We have a long way to go tomorrow.'

Degannwy, our destination, lies on the coast north of Powys, in the kingdom of Gwynedd. We could either keep to the east of the mountains and follow the course of the river Hafren, or cross the river by ferry, follow the south coast road from Dinas Powys, and turn north by the roads the Romans had built, riding through the mountains. It was hard going, but the beauty of the countryside kept up my spirits. We stopped to eat where the road was flanked with great rough-hewn stones, set upright in the ground, like the standing stones on the moors at home; but these were carved with strange signs. I asked Myrddin what they were.

'*Ogam*,' he replied, 'the writing my people use for inscriptions on stone. Straight lines are easier to carve with a hammer and chisel than curved ones. These commemorate dead heroes. We're nearing the crossroads. We must turn westward and find the coast road. I hope the weather holds.'

The weather did not hold. We were forced to take shelter in a cave while the rain beat down and thunder crashed over our heads. The horses were terrified. Gorvenal lit a fire, grumbling all the time about 'ladylike poets' who delighted in leading honest soldiers over mountains in order to soak them to the skin. The storm showed no signs of abating. We each had our emergency rations and a blanket with us, so we ate a little dried meat and decided to turn in, and hope for an early start tomorrow. I couldn't sleep. I asked Myrddin to play to me. He played a little and then murmured, 'I'll recite something I wrote for my wife when we were first married.'

I had only heard his public performances before, when he declaimed about battles and heroes; but now he told of flowers and grasses, and his wife's hair and her breasts, and the secrets of his heart. Tears filled my throat. I looked down at my clumsy calloused hands. I'd never be a poet like him. Full of woe, I slept . . .

We woke to a clear dawn with frost in the air. After a quick meal and a drink of icy spring water, we set off. The horses were well rested and Myrddin set as fast a pace as possible. He didn't talk to either of us, but rode in front looking stern. The weather seemed likely to remain good, but he was taking no chances. We didn't want to spend another night out. In the afternoon, however, Gorvenal's mare went lame. I think she had stumbled during the morning and the fast going had worsened the sprain. We had to lead her, and Gorvenal took turns riding behind me and Myrddin.

It was almost dark by the time we limped into the hermitage; they told us it was called Llanddewi-Brefi. It was a mean place, just a collection of round huts perched there in the cleft of the mountain. The hermits looked half-starved and were dressed in rags with gleaming shaven foreheads and matted locks. However, they received us kindly, and gave us bowls of thick vegetable stew and let us sleep on the floor of one of the huts. The smell turned my stomach.

'Great Mithras,' began Gorvenal, clasping his hands in mock prayer, 'grant that that good-for-nothing mare is better tomorrow. Don't condemn us to spend more than one night in this stable.'

'You should pray to Christ,' said Myrddin seriously, propping himself up on one elbow on his pile of straw. 'This is his place.'

Gorvenal went to put a cold compress on his mare's leg. Either this, or his prayer, or both, worked, for the mare was fit in the morning. That day we managed to get to Towyn, sleeping the night in a fisherman's hut, and arrived filthy and travel-worn at the fortress of Degannwy on the evening of the eighth day since we set out from Castle Dor.

# Six

We had left Gorvenal in the care of Blodwyn the cook back at the palace, and I'd come on alone with Myrddin.

'Here is my house,' he said. 'You are welcome, Drustan.'

A servant opened the door and a tall woman with golden hair came forward. When she saw Myrddin she gave a low cry of joy and threw herself into his arms. 'I've been anxious,' she said. 'There's been no word for so long. Oh Myrddin —'

I was wondering whether I would be able to find my way back to the palace, when a man's voice said, 'Where are you going?' and I turned round.

Another man had come out of the house. He was stockily built, with curly hair, and he carried a year old child.

'Gwion!' Myrddin cried, and they embraced.

The woman took the child.

Gwion said, 'You had forgotten your companion, Myrddin. He was ready to run away.'

Myrddin took my arm. 'I'm sorry, Drustan, come inside. I haven't seen my wife for so long, and my daughter was only a baby when I left. I can hardly believe she's grown so.'

The child clung to her mother and wouldn't look at him. We went inside and the servant brought wine. As we drank Myrddin told them of his travels, and Gwion questioned him about King Arthur's expedition against Lancelin.

Gwion asked, 'And the boy?'

'Drustan is going to Môn.'

'Indeed?' smiled Gwion, and gave me a quizzical look. 'You're following in our footsteps?'

'Are you a bard too?' I asked him eagerly, but before he could reply Myrddin said, 'There'll be plenty of time to talk later. We must wash, Drustan, and then we can eat. I'm sure you're as hungry as I am.'

Myrddin gave me one of his tunics to wear. I kept close to him as a dog does to its master. I felt he was so much my superior in every way. After supper we sat round the fire and talked, and I tried to ask them questions about Ynys Môn, but they were exultant after their reunion, and wouldn't be serious.

'While you've been away,' Gwion said, 'the court's been crowded with bards, attracted more by the news of King Maelgwn's generosity than by dedication to their art. Well, at last I had enough of it. I put a spell on them. Whenever one of them opened his mouth to recite all he could do was make a noise like a baby with his finger on his lips: *blewrm*, *blewrm*! Apart from that I've made songs . . . sometimes . . . What's the use? Who listens? And you?'

'I gave them what they wanted,' Myrddin said.

'Before you go to the druids,' Gwion said, 'you will need the blessing of King Maelgwn.'

'And,' said Myrddin, 'you will have to spend a night in the druids' cave.' I asked him to explain. 'Once,' he said, 'bards went there in search of inspiration, now it's said to be haunted. Men may be told their future if they do what the spirits ask.'

Suddenly the firelight flickered and faded, the lamps burned down, I felt a chill like hunger and cold, and I remembered Cerridwen's warning.

'What is it, Drustan?' asked Gwion. 'Are you afraid?'

'No,' I said. 'No. There is little use in being afraid.'

The great King Maelgwn gave me his blessing and a small purse of gold. A messenger was sent to Môn. And then it was time for me to go to the cave.

I sat in the dark as near to the entrance as I could. The soldiers had blocked it with a boulder which they would roll away in the morning, but through the aperture I could see a few stars, clear as milk, high above me.

I had no food with me and no light, only a flask of water

34

and my sword. I began to doze as the night wore on, roused now and again by a soft wailing close at hand which might have been the wind, but was not. Then suddenly I was wide awake. The wailing was louder now and seemed to fill the cave. I leaped to my feet. It was the darkest part of the night, just before dawn, and voices were calling me, 'Drustan, Drustan, Drustan . . .'

My voice broke in the silence, and I cleared my throat. 'What do you want?'

No answer, but the same moaning, 'Drustan, Drustan, Drustan . . .'

'If you have some message for me, speak!'

What was it they cried? 'Give us water for glad news, give us blood for a warning.'

'Water,' I said, 'I have water.' My throat was dry with fear, but I poured the contents of my flask on to the ground. 'Here is water.'

'You shall not lack love, love of men and women, both shall be yours.'

'You shall not lack children. Sons and daughters will be born to you.'

'You shall not lack honour. Kings shall give you presents.'

The voices subsided, sighing into the depths of the cave.

'What more?' I said.

'Blood for a warning.'

'You shall have it.' Gritting my teeth I drew my sword blade up my arm. Drops of blood dripped on to the ground. Immediately a roar like a great gale filled the cave and I dropped to my knees, covering my ears with my hands.

'Oh gods!' I cried. 'Are there so many warnings?'

I could scarcely hear, but some voices reached me more clearly than others through the dreadful din.

'Beware of the princess from the sea.'

'Beware of a cousin who is no kin.'

'Beware of a land of mists and snow. Friends lost there are lost forever.'

'Beware of a golden potion in a cup of gold.'

There was more, much more, but I covered my ears so I should not hear it all.

When the soldiers rolled away the stone I saw that Myrddin and Gwion had come to take me home.

'Well?' said Gwion, after a glance at his friend. 'What did you hear?'

'Groaning and voices,' I said. 'Nothing more. What did you think I would hear?'

'We told you,' said Myrddin gently, 'some have had their fate foretold by the spirits . . . But you heard nothing?' He was looking at the cut on my arm.

'Nothing,' I said.

Myrddin came with me to the boat. We reined in our horses at the top of the cliff and stared across to the island over the water, which showed purple and creamy white. On the beach was a large rowing boat, manned by hooded oarsmen. They sat impassively and did not speak to each other.

Myrddin pointed across the water. 'There is Môn.'

'I wish you could come with me,' I said. He did not answer. 'You could come if you wanted, couldn't you?' I persisted, like a child who is over-tired, trying to extract some all-important, meaningless affirmative.

'If I wanted,' he said wearily, 'yes. But I have other things to do, Drustan, than to come with you.'

I turned away to hide my face. 'But you said —'

His expression hardened. 'Look, Drustan, we've been friends. I've done you a favour. In return I've had your companionship on a journey that would otherwise have been tedious, but that doesn't mean that I'll change my life in obedience to some childish whim of yours.'

'But you said — ever since that first evening at Castle Dor it has haunted me — *It is death to mock a poet, death to love a poet, death to be a poet.*'

'Don't quote my words back to me,' he said. 'I'm not one to be kept in the cage of relationships.'

I left him there on the cliff top, slid down the path and helped them push out the boat. I took a pair of oars myself. Myrddin remained on the cliff, his cloak flapping in the wind. He raised his arm once and waved uncertainly.

36

# Seven

I tried to give myself wholly to the druids, to cleanse my mind of my memories and my desires, to absorb their ancient learning, their lore, but some part of me would not be humbled; it stood aside and mocked and longed for Myrddin and the world beyond the sacred island. I did learn to play the harp and recite the old songs and to make new songs of my own, but I could never do magic, as some of the others did, and I knew that this was because my will was unsubdued. This was what I wanted above all, because of Cerridwen, and I told myself that one day I would succeed. Meanwhile, it made me bitter and envious, and I was not well liked.

One evening in my third year on Ynys Môn I was out on the cliffs, alone as usual. I stood in the biting wind staring at the turbulent sea, my thoughts tumultuous and rebellious as the waves, fighting, fighting against my fate. Never to be king of Leones: to wander the earth. . . .

I began picking up great pieces of stone from the cliff top and hurling them with all my strength into the sea. I heard a shout behind me, 'Hey, you madman! What are you doing?'

It was one of the boys from my class. He thumbed his nose derisively.

I caught him round the knees in a running tackle and he fell with a thump. I tried to get an arm lock on him but he was too quick; he writhed out of my grasp, and then twisted backwards so he had me with his forearm against my throat. In the next few moments, as I battled for breath, it became apparent that he knew what he was about. He might be smaller, but he was wiry, and quicker too. I would need all my extra weight. I forced up his arm and we rolled over and over on the grass, both of us already short of wind.

We fought with grim joy until it grew dark. Then exhausted, we lay panting side by side.

'I wanted to kill you,' I said when I could speak.

'I don't care,' he said. 'That's the best fight I've ever had. Who was your master?'

'Gorvenal the veteran.'

'My brother taught me. Morholt, his name is. I'd give anything for a practice bout with Morholt now, just one. Then I'd show you.'

'Come up here tomorrow,' I said, 'and try again.'

The boy I fought with had bright red hair. His name was Brendan and he and his brother Morholt were the nephews of King Angus of Laighin, a kingdom in the southeast of Erin.

The island and the peaceful, self-denying world of the druids held me like a cage. I must have the key, and escape. All this time I had had no word of my father, and I had ceased to look for Myrddin when the boat came over from the mainland; but in the autumn of my third year news of a different kind reached us. There was war in Lloegrys, not between King Arthur and the Saxons, but civil war. His own natural son, Modred, had seized Gwenhyvaer, Arthur's queen, and they were now besieged by Arthur at Camlon.

I made a plan. I would go to Degannwy and try to find Myrddin or Gorvenal, and persuade them to come with me. But if need be I would ride south alone, and join King Arthur's forces.

The next morning I slipped away early, took one of the fishing boats and rowed across to the mainland. My wrestling bouts with Brendan had stood me in good stead. I said goodbye to no one.

I began the walk to Degannwy. I still couldn't believe that I was leaving Môn. I expected them to come up behind me suddenly on horses and take me back. About noon a farmer gave me a lift on his cart and drove me the rest of the way. Whatever happened I knew I had no time to waste; but I couldn't resist the temptation to linger as I entered the gates of Degannwy once more, for I had seen nothing of the outside world for so long. Degannwy seemed much less magnificent, and I realised that my time with the druids had changed me more than I knew.

I made for Myrddin's house, but when I knocked the servant who opened the door told me that his master was away in the north. He asked if I would speak to the lady Nefydd. I declined. There was nothing she could tell me. Then a thought struck me. I turned back. 'Wait, lord Myrddin's friend, the bard Gwion, is he here?'

'Assuredly, lord. You'll find him in the king's hall.'

I thanked him and made my way towards the centre of the town, trying to decide what to do. I might be wasting my time; on the other hand Gwion might be able to give me valuable information. Curiosity got the better of me, and hunger too. I went into the hall and sat at the bottom of the lowest table, the hood of my cloak pulled up round my chin. I had a good meal, and just as I was finishing I saw Gwion come in. He sat down quite near me and began to drink steadily. From his seat far away at the top of the table, King Maelgwn of Gwynedd gave the sign and a bard stepped forward. He was gaudily dressed and wore a small beard trimmed into a fork at the end. I could tell that he had no idea what he was about. He went on for some time. I glanced at Gwion. He was grinning cynically and draining another cup of ale.

At last his turn came. He stood up, marched to the front of the hall and bowed to the king, and then, ironically, to the other bard, who gave him a haughty smile.

> I am a stag: *of seven tines,*
> I am a flood: *across a plain,*
> I am a wind: *on a deep lake,*
> I am a tear: *the Sun lets fall,*
> I am a hawk: *above the cliff,*
> I am a thorn: *beneath the nail,*
> I am a wonder: *among flowers,*
> I am a wizard: *who but I*
> *Sets the cool head aflame with smoke?*

I am a spear: *that roars for blood,*
I am a salmon: *in a pool,*
I am a lure: *from paradise,*
I am a hill: *where poets walk,*
I am a boar: *renowned and red,*
I am a breaker: *threatening doom,*
I am a tide: *that drags to death,*
I am an infant: *who but I*
*Peeps from the unhewn dolmen arch?*

I am the womb: *of every holt,*
I am the blaze: *on every hill,*
I am the queen: *of every hive*
I am the shield: *for every head*
I am the grave: *of every hope.*

There was dead silence when he had finished. The other bard had gone very red. 'Well?' Gwion asked. 'Can you tell me the answer?' Nobody spoke. The king drummed his fingers impatiently on the arm of his chair. 'The answer,' said Gwion, 'is the god Apollo.'

'Your poetry is obscure,' said the king. He gave Gwion nothing.

Gwion went back to his seat and picked up his cup again. By this time I'd eaten my fill and drunk enough; I got up, tapped Gwion on the shoulder and spoke his name. He turned, half-laughing, half-angry at being interrupted.

'Good evening,' I said.

'Well? What can I do for you?'

'I came to find Myrddin,' I explained, 'but his servant told me he's gone north. I wondered if you could help me.'

'Maybe,' he said, getting up from the table. 'Come over here where we can talk quietly.'

Another pseudo-bard had begun his boring and inept song. Gwion led me to a bench against the wall, found me a cup of ale, and drew me down beside him. He looked tired, bitter.

'Tell me your name and what I can do for you.'

'My name is Drustan. Myrddin brought me here three years ago from Kernow, and I met you at his house.'

His face broke into a smile. 'Of course! I remember you, but now you are grown. Have you just come from Môn?'

I nodded. 'News reached us of Arthur.'

'And you're riding south? Why?'

'My duty.'

'Duty?' He shrugged.

'When will Myrddin be back?'

'Who knows? Myrddin's like the wind. It's impossible to hold him.'

'I know,' I said ruefully.

He smiled at me and said more gently, 'He'll be back. Must you go south? Why not stay here and wait for him?'

I looked at him: he was Myrddin's friend. I had just spent three years alone, and I was planning a hard ride without a companion to a battle not mine, for a king I knew only from the tales of others. I was half tempted. He took my arm. 'Why rush to your fate?' he said. 'It will come to find you soon enough.'

'Because that's my nature,' I said.

I embraced him and went to find Blodwyn the cook.

She, at length and with many tears, disclosed that Gorvenal had left for Kernow soon after I went to Môn, and had never returned. She showed me a sleeping child, about two years old, which she claimed was his; and there was a strong resemblance to him in its squat little face.

I had not really expected to find Gorvenal still at Degannwy. I wrapped myself in my cloak and lay down in a warm corner of the kitchen to sleep. I was reconciled to going on alone, but not to going on foot.

I woke before dawn and went to the stables. The grooms were still asleep. I examined the horses and picked out a good-looking one. Taking his saddle and bridle from the nail in his stall I led him outside, willing him not to make a noise. As I strapped on the gear I recognised him; it was King Maelgwn's own horse, Traitor's Bane.

I swung myself into the saddle. Best to put a bold face on it. I rode towards the gates. The sentries were drowsing at their posts, and it was little more than half light. I dug my heels into the horse's flanks.

'Open up!' I shouted, sweating with fear. 'Hurry! I've an urgent message from the king!'

One of the guards began slowly to unbar the gates. He cursed steadily. Traitor's Bane cavorted in the roadway. He sensed my fear: he too was anxious to be off. At last the gates were open. He needed no urging from me, he went like the wind. He cleared the ditches, soaring like a bird. I clung on to his back as if I had never sat on a horse before, but that was no matter, on the journey south I'd have plenty of practice.

# *Eight*

It took me four days. I went the easy way along the river
Hafren. The roads were bad, winter was coming. But I met
no enemies: Saxons, brigands, or Maelgwn of Gwynedd's
troops. Everywhere I stopped, the news was the same:
Arthur's army was encamped before Camlon, battle had
not been joined, Modred would not surrender. I laughed at
myself sometimes, a lone man on his way to rescue a king.
After those soft years on Môn it was good to feel a horse
between my thighs. I had no sword, no shield, no armour.
Traitor's Bane seemed tireless.

Then at Aquae Sulis, where I had to pause the last night
at an inn, they told me the news: *Arthur is dead.* Modred
had killed him treacherously when they met for a parley.
Arthur is dead . . .

I ate and slept, and in the morning rode on to Camlon. It
was true. Less than half way on the road I began to meet
refugees, survivors escaping from the scene of the battle,
and a few mercenaries returning home with their quickly
snatched spoil.

I rode across the plain in front of the fortress, where, I
suppose, the meeting between Arthur and Modred had
taken place. It was littered with corpses, among them
bodies which still twitched and groaned. Within the walls
the dead lay in their own blood. Women wailed. I led
Traitor's Bane away. I realised I was very tired, and it was
dangerous to stay; I was unarmed and the horse made a
tempting prize.

I tethered him in a near-by coppice. During the journey
we had become good friends and I laid my head on his neck

43

and wept. I had never seen the scourges of war before and I was sickened.

Presently I heard the steady thud of approaching hoof-beats. I dried my tears on my hair and listened. A large band of riders seemed to be coming my way. I led Traitor's Bane out of the trees, mounted, and rode to meet them. Before we had covered half the ground I was kicking my heels into his flanks and yelling with delight. At the head of the troop rode my father.

We leapt from our horses and fell into each other's arms.

'Drustan! You, here, by all the gods!' he panted. 'I might have known no son of mine could keep from this battle.'

'We're too late,' I said. 'The battle's over. Arthur's slain.'

His face darkened. 'Have you seen him?'

'No, but I —'

'We must find out for sure. Rohalt!' he called to one of his lords, 'follow us to the fortress but keep the men outside. If you hear the alarum come to our aid. Hywel, come with us.'

For the first time I recognised my old friend. He had let his moustache grow, but the broad smile he gave me hadn't changed. We rode off towards the fortress, shouting questons to and fro, but hardly catching the answers. Now that I had companions I could endure the ghastly sights and sounds without flinching. We rode up to the gates and dismounted, leaving our horses with the men. Cynmor threw his arm round my shoulders and held me to him briefly, then, with me on his left — his shield arm — and Hywel at his right, we passed through the half-open gateway.

There was a pyre in the yard, and the smoke caught me by the throat. They'd started to burn the dead. A gaggle of weeping women were clustered round. Cynmor demanded of them the whereabouts of Arthur. One turned on him, red-eyed and as shrill as a fury.

'Arthur's corpse, you mean,' she cried, 'for Arthur is no more. In the tower room, that's where they took him.'

Another said, 'Curse the day that ever the traitor Modred was got!'

We went to the tower room. At the top of the steps Cynmor drew his sword and knocked with its hilt on the doorpost.

There was a long silence, then a low voice asked, 'Who knocks?'

'Cynmor, King of Leones.'

Again a silence, then, so low that we hardly heard, 'Enter.'

On a stone bench that ran the length of the wall lay the dead body of King Arthur. I knelt beside him and wept that it was too late now for me ever to know him. His spirit had long since departed, and I saw but a corpse, pale, noble, at rest. They had washed the blood from him and closed his eyes.

The living, clustered round a table in the centre of the room, turned to face us: the queen, no longer young, no longer beautiful, but still possessed of the dignity which her position had lent her. The young man, sallow and sullen, twisting his fingers together. And the old soldier, striving to master his grief with years of professional discipline.

'I trust,' said the queen, 'that you have not come here with any treacherous intent, King Cynmor.'

She knew that it would be an easy matter for my father to slaughter the remnants of both armies and to take the fortress for his own.

'Lady, do not fear,' said Cynmor. 'I had hoped to bring assistance to the king. I am very grieved that I have come too late.'

'It wasn't my fault!' Modred burst out. 'Believe me, I didn't do it! . . . They're all saying that I killed him by a trick, but I didn't plan it, I swear I didn't. That soldier drew his sword because a snake stung him on the foot. The men took it as a sign, and before I could stop —'

'Keep silence, Modred,' said the queen. 'Have you no pride?' Then, as tears mastered her, '. . . You have your way . . . he's dead now. He's dead.' She stood up. 'Lord,' she said to my father, 'I'm leaving this place. Please arrange an escort to take me to the religious house at Treames. I will go now and make ready.'

45

She went out, and I thought, even if every one of the evil tales about her is true, she is still worthy to have been Arthur's queen.

'Damn her!' Modred said softly. 'Why did she refuse to marry me? But I don't need her. . . . I'll *still* be king.'

'Lord,' said the old soldier, 'I am Bedwyr. It was the king's wish that his body should be taken to Ynys Witrin. I have sent a message to the people on the island. A boat will be waiting this evening at the crossing. You must pardon me, I was wounded. It's nothing, but —'

'I'll see to it,' I said.

'I have a mission of my own to fulfil. His sword, Excalibur. He did not wish it to fall into other hands.' Bedwyr looked at Modred.

Modred returned a glance full of hatred.

Before noon the queen left for Treames with an armed escort led by Rohalt, and my father set out under cover with Bedwyr, who carried King Arthur's sword in his own scabbard. Before he went, Cynmor had the king's body brought down from the tower room and placed in the back of a small covered cart. We draped it with purple and all the rich cloth we could find. There was not much time. Cynmor told Hywel and me to drive slowly along the road to Ynys Witrin, and when he had seen Bedwyr back to Camlon in safety, he would come after us. The veteran was in pain, he could scarcely sit on his horse, but he wouldn't hear of entrusting his mission to anyone else.

But when evening came we had almost reached the island, and it seemed clear that my father was not going to arrive in time. We stopped and the small band of soldiers that accompanied us lit a fire and cooked some food. Hywel and I talked quietly of the past. I told him a little about life on Ynys Môn, then we fell silent. I had a word with the soldiers, telling them to remain where they were until we returned, then I went back to Hywel.

'We'd better be going,' I said. 'It's almost dark.'

Hywel took the cart along the last straight mile of road and up the gentle curve of the hill that enfolds the lake of Ynys Witrin like a hand holding a cup. We could hear the lapping of the marsh water. Logs had been laid from the end of the track to the water's edge, and between them the mud sucked and oozed. I knew Hywel, too, was frightened.

'Stay with the cart,' I said. 'I'll see if anyone's there.'

He climbed down and stood holding the horses' heads. They nuzzled him and whinnied softly. I went gingerly down to the lake, hearing the mud squelch under my boots and wished I'd thought to bring a lantern. The sun was set but the moon had not yet risen. It was quite dark.

I heard the approaching boat before I saw it.

It was coming towards me out of the darkness. The water slapped gently against the sides; a low throaty chanting and a high faint humming seemed to ebb and flow with the movement of the water. The one who punted the boat had a lantern set in front of him on the prow. Three hooded figures sat in the boat. The fourth brought it in to the bank, and I ran to hold the side steady. The three alighted on the shore. All were women, as I could tell by the cold slender hands that they reached out as I helped each one from the boat; but for the rest, they were muffled in long black robes, with hoods to shield their faces. The foremost spoke to me.

'Where is Bedwyr?'

'He had an errand to perform for the king. I came instead. I am Drustan of Leones.'

'We have heard of you, Drustan. I am Queen Morgana, Arthur's sister. Have you no men with you?'

'I told them to stay at the end of the road. It seemed more fitting. My friend and I brought King Arthur's bier to the lake-side.'

'You have a poet's soul.' Her hood had fallen back a little. I saw black hair, bound with pearls, and a noble, sensuous face. 'Fate chose wisely when she chose you for his escort. You will not forget this day.'

'No, lady,' I said.

One of her companions stepped forward. 'Lady . . . ?'

Morgana pulled back the hood that covered her bright

47

hair and fair young face. 'This is Nimue, the lady of the lake. Don't look too long, Drustan, she is not for you.'

The girl blushed.

Then the third hooded lady turned her face towards me, and I almost cried out, for she was as white as a leper and as gaunt as a skull. 'Where is he?' she asked through cracked lips. 'We have come here to fetch him, not to talk.'

'The Queen of the Waste Lands,' said Morgana to me, and her voice held a note of fear. 'Go and bring my brother's corpse. It doesn't do to keep her waiting.'

I stumbled back up the bank. One look at my face was enough for Hywel. We went round to the back of the cart and opened the flaps. The moon was rising now, and by her light I could see Arthur's face. For a moment I hesitated. It seemed better to dig a hole in the ground and put him in it, than hand him over to those fearsome women. But this was my task.

We got him down as best we could and carried the board he lay on to the water's edge. The hermit helped us put him into the boat. Then the three queens went aboard. The hag first, then the virgin and last Morgana. She turned in the stern and raised her hand to me. Hywel and I helped the hermit to push off the now laden boat, and his pole bit through the still black marsh water as he began the weary crossing.

The Queen of the Waste Lands resumed her slow throaty chanting, and Nimue answered her in a voice higher and clearer than a boy's. Morgana had opened her robe to show a long scarlet tunic.

'Look for us again!' she called across the water.

We didn't reach Camlon till after midnight, and everyone seemed drunk. I tried to ask for news of my father or Bedwyr, but nobody could answer sensibly. I dismissed the troop. Hywel told me to rouse him if I should need him, and then went off by himself saying that he must get some sleep. I was too anxious to be sleepy, so I went up to the tower room.

48

Modred was sitting slumped forward on the table, with his hair in a pool of wine. Beside him sat Cynmor.

'Father!'

He looked up at me.

I had always thought of him as being in the flower of his strength, but now suddenly I saw he was an ageing man. His face was deeply furrowed with lines and old scars, and his hair had long fingers of grey at the temples. 'Father . . .' I said.

His hand reached out, gripped my arm, and drew me down beside him. 'Oh gods, Drustan,' he said. 'I've seen such things . . . I can't begin to describe . . . But tell me, did you take his body to the lake-side? What happened?'

I told him everything. 'But father, it's only just struck me . . . the tor on Ynys Witrin is the highest point for miles around, isn't it?' He nodded. 'Well, I couldn't see it. There were no landmarks, almost as if the lake met the sea out there. And the moon had risen quite high by the time we came away. The lake's not all that wide, is it?'

'No. A tall man could wade it, except when the rains have been very heavy.'

We were silent for some time, each drinking, lost in our separate thoughts.

'Well, he's gone,' Cynmor said at last. 'We'd better go to bed. There's a lot to do tomorrow. This sot' – with a contemptuous thumb cocked at Modred – 'is no more use than a suckling babe.'

'Father,' I said, 'what did you see? And where's Bedwyr?'

'Bedwyr is dead,' said Cynmor shortly. 'He had a wound in the belly, the ride was too much for him.'

'I'm a man,' I said, 'don't treat me like a child.'

'Arthur's sword was no common one. When he knew he was dying he gave it to Bedwyr and made him promise to throw it in the lake, where it came from.'

'The lake?'

'The same lake of Ynys Witrin. But swear you'll tell no one, Drustan, I'm breaking my oath telling you this. That's why we had to be so careful to avoid you on the road.' He broke off. 'I suppose Modred *is* out cold?'

I kicked him, he didn't stir.

'Let's get outside anyhow. I'm sick of this room. It smells of death.'

Outside the yard was still. Cynmor leaned on my shoulder.

'We got to the lake-side, a secluded part, hidden by trees. Bedwyr was pretty far gone, he had to lie down on the bank. He gave me the sword and told me to throw it in. I stood by the water. Of course, you never saw Excalibur, a beautifully balanced sword with a king's ransom in the hilt. It seemed a crime to throw it in, so I just hid it among the reeds. I thought, I can collect it later. I'm not trying to excuse —'

'Go on,' I said.

'So I went back to Bedwyr and told him I'd done as he asked. "What happened?" he said. "Nothing," I said. "What did you expect to happen?" "Go and throw the sword into the water," he said. "Can't you see I'm dying? How will I face my lord Christ and King Arthur if I haven't done his bidding?" '

'Was Bedwyr a Christian, too?'

'Looks like it.'

'What happened then?'

'I went back and pulled Excalibur out of the reeds. The blade was stained with mud. I thought, it must be true. The sword does give victory. And I . . . I thought . . . What couldn't *I* do with a sword like this? So I hid it under a tree root and went back again. Bedwyr was bleeding fast and his eyes couldn't focus on me. "I've done what you asked," I said. "What happened?" he whispered again. "The water lapped," I said. "The sun's shining. A king-fisher flew out of the bush —" "Curse you!" he screamed. "How can you cheat a dying man?" His breath came out with a terrific rattle. I thought, he's had it now, but I was ashamed. I pelted down the bank, snatched the sword from under the root, and threw it as hard as I could out over the water, and . . .' he stopped.

'And?'

'Drustan, these years I've been married to Cerridwen,

I've seen magic done, you know. She's a witch, she can do things you and I can't, so I know that —'

'The druids are also magicians,' I said. 'I know a little of the hidden workings of nature. What happened?'

'As I threw the sword it curved over the water in a perfect arc, and then a hand reached up out of the lake.'

'*A hand?*'

'Yes, and an arm, shining like silver. And this, this *hand* caught Excalibur by the hilt and brandished it, and then drew it down beneath the water. I went back to Bedwyr and told him what I thought I'd seen. I think he heard me . . . He must have done. He smiled and said, "Thank you. Then it's accomplished," and he died. Drustan, I did see it. I *think* I saw it. I was dead tired, but I wasn't drunk. I haven't got a fever.'

I smiled at him as best I could. 'Hywel and I saw the Hooded Three tonight.'

'Who?'

'Queen Morgana, Arthur's sister, and her ladies. But they were robed in black. They were the Hooded Three all right.'

My words seemed to disturb him more than what he himself had just said. He blinked at me anxiously. 'It's almost morning,' I said. 'Come to bed.'

'Drustan,' Cynmor said, 'you *believe* me, don't you?' He sounded surprised.

'Of course I believe you,' I said, 'I'm a poet, remember?' and I kissed him.

# Nine

With King Arthur and Bedwyr gone and most of the best men dead in battle, Modred seemed determined to rule with a clique of his own supporters.

'King Mark will be angry,' said Cynmor.

If Modred's uncertain rule laid him open to attack, not only Lloegrys but the whole of Kernow would be in jeopardy.

'If only Lancelin would come back,' my father went on, 'he could save Lloegrys.'

But rumour reached us that Lancelin had gone into a religious house in Armorica. With uneasy hearts we travelled back to Kanoel.

Kanoel, at least was unchanged: windswept, gaunt, with a savage beauty all its own. I was so glad to see my home once more that even the first terror of meeting Cerridwen passed, and I thought how strange it was that the years that had brought me to manhood had seemed not to touch her. She looked just the same as she had that day when she had stepped off the ship arrayed in ancient finery, to be married to my father. She had given Cynmor no more children, but their three sons, Kiaran, Set and Ganny were growing up well and strong.

At first I avoided her, and I was often lonely. The winter closed in, but I spent long days re-exploring the cliffs and caves that I had discovered in childhood. At night I would make songs and play a little. About the time of the Midwinter Festival, Hywel told me that he had decided to marry in the spring.

'Aigfu is a Christian,' he told me. 'While you were away a monk came to Kanoel. His name was Paul Aurelian.'

'Were you baptized too?'

He nodded.

I saw less of Hywel after his marriage and missed his companionship. My father was for the most part away. Bands of pirates from Erin had taken to braving the weather and making raids on our coast. I was always alone.

Hywel said to me, 'Haven't you got a girl, Drustan? One you'd like to marry, I mean.'

Aigfu had conceived a child, and he seemed tranquil and mature. I think he suspected me of having a mistress, some slave girl I was ashamed to be seen with.

'No,' I said, 'I haven't got a girl.'

I began to think about women, but there was no one that I wanted to touch.

Cerridwen asked me to teach her some songs. 'I know only those I learned as a child,' she said, 'and they're all sad songs. Teach me something gay.'

I taught her a little druidic song about the coming of spring, and after that we would sometimes sing it together. She played some pipes that she had brought with her when she was married, and I a harp that had also come from the Islands of the Dead.

It seemed that the dark side of her was eclipsed. I could not forget the time she had tried to poison me, but it seemed like a different life and two different people, so unreal had my memories become. And yet it had happened. One day she spoke of it.

'Do you ever think of the poison cup now?' she asked.

I was tuning a string that had loosened. I plucked it, putting my ear close to the harp. 'Sometimes,' I said. 'For a long while after, I was afraid of you. That's why I went away to Môn, but now I've grown up the fear's passed. You don't still hate me, do you?'

'No. Since you were with the druids you've changed. What magic did you learn?'

We talked of technical things for a while. We were in the orchard outside the gates of Kanoel, and the sun poured down through the leaves. It seemed strange to be discussing magic, and the powers of destruction and hate.

Cerridwen stretched, and laid her veil on the grass. 'Sometimes,' she said, 'I'm not a witch at all. Sometimes, when I'm with the children or with you, here, now . . . the sun and the flowers make me happy and content. No need to *do* anything. But sometimes,' her face grew tense, 'I feel this terrible *will*. It seems to surge up inside me and burst in my head. I'm possessed: I know then that I've got the power to *make something happen*. Whatever I want. To destroy. And when it's over I feel peaceful again, but some creature has died.' She broke off. 'That's what happened that day . . . with you . . . but I couldn't go on with it. If I had really *willed*, you know, you'd be dead.'

'I owe you my life then,' I said as lightly as I could, 'as if you were my mother . . . my real mother died when I was born . . . I wonder if *she* hates me.'

We sat for some time in silence, then Cerridwen said, 'Drustan, do you ever wish you were king?'

'King?'

'King of this kingdom. And my husband.'

I looked at her hand. The fingers were covered with earth. She'd been digging them deep into the grass. In a moment everything was changed, and even before I looked at her face, I knew.

In the orchard the birds seemed to stop singing and the sun grew dark. I was filled with desire. My eyes couldn't believe that she stood up and unpinned her dress, so that her body blazed white and black and red among the trees. I held her against the trunk of a tree, for I felt that we were both drowning, and I kissed her on the mouth, deep into her mouth, as if by that alone I could possess her.

'Cerridwen, Cerridwen,' I said, 'I never realised, I never knew.'

'I knew,' she said.

Then, as I held her against me, she began to talk, so quickly and fluently that I knew her speech was the result of many nights lying sleepless in the dark, sleepless beside my father. She told me that she had always wanted me, but fought to conquer her desire. She said she was glad when I went away, for she had some rest, but when I came back it was twice as bad as before, because now I was a grown man, tall and strong. She ran her hands over my body. I wanted to throw her down on the grass and take her as I had once seen a stallion mount a mare, quickly and brutally, but her voice went on and on, and at last I realised what it was she was saying.

'If he died, you see, you could have me *and* Leones. He isn't young any more. We can't go back to the Islands of the Dead. He'd come after us with an army. He'd never let us live in peace. He must die. But I can do it, I'll do it for you, Drustan, and then you'll be king, I'll be your wife, we'll be together . . .'

My body grew cold. I was shaking. I thrust her from me on to the grass, but now her body, which had appeared so beautiful, seemed flabby and disgusting. I threw her her dress. 'Put that on,' I said.

I felt sick. I sat down with my back to her. The fall had winded her and I could hear her fighting to get her breath.

'The answer's no,' I said. I wanted to hurt her more, but I couldn't bear the thought of touching her.

She glanced at me and struggled into her dress, panting. Once, I think it was my first hunt, I had got a doe at bay, surrounded by dogs. Cerridwen made me remember that. The dogs had torn the doe to pieces. The hate went out of me suddenly and I was left only with self-loathing and a bitter taste on my tongue.

'What will you do?' she said dully.

'Go away. Leave you in peace.'

'I don't want peace,' she said. 'Don't go. You'll kill me, Drustan.'

'Rather that than kill my father. Cerridwen, why do you hate him? He's always been kind to you.'

'Because I had no choice,' she said, 'no choice in the marriage.' She got up slowly, dressed now, her veil hiding her hair. 'I was stupid to speak,' she said. 'I should have waited. If you had once lain with me you would not have

56

been able to leave me. But the words had been burning my tongue for so long. Oh Drustan —'

'Don't speak any more,' I said.

I saw her teeth come down on her lower lip, which grew white with pressure, and then blood stained it red again. Fear and hatred fought with pity in me.

'Cerridwen,' I said, 'please love him.'

I was young then. I thought, it's a kind of sickness. Time will heal her. 'Don't think of me any more,' I said.

If she had succeeded with her poison cup while I was still a child, she couldn't have banished me from Kanoel more surely. The second cup she offered me was more deadly than the first, because I was thirsty for it. I knew I'd never sleep another night at Kanoel after the first, when I lay awake, remembering each detail of her body in the orchard, and dozed only to dream of embracing her.

The following morning I sought out Cynmor. She had told him that she was sick, and was keeping to her rooms. According to the plan that had formed in my aching head towards dawn, I said I'd decided to go to Castle Dor. If the rumours we had heard were true, King Mark was also troubled by raiding parties from Erin, and he might have some work for me. I pointed out that I hadn't yet proved myself in battle.

Cynmor heard me to the end without a word, then he said, 'It's all true, Drustan, all true, but must you go?'

'My mind's made up, father,' I said.

'Take Gorvenal, then, he'll look after you if anyone can. And come back soon.'

I said goodbye to Hywel and his wife, and Gorvenal and I set off the same day. As we drew away from Kanoel my heart lightened a little. Traitor's Bane was going beautifully, glad to be on the road again.

'There's more to this trip than you're telling, isn't there, lord?' asked Gorvenal after we had ridden for some miles in silence.

'Keep your mouth shut,' I said, 'or go home.'

'Abuse me if you like,' Gorvenal said, 'but I know what's

happened, and so would Cynmor if he kept his eyes open. Don't feel too bad about having had her, lad. You're not the first, you know.'

Then I wished that I had killed her, but it was too late. I managed to ask, 'Does everyone know?'

'No. She's careful, I'll give her that. But Breisa's one of her maids now, you see.'

I dug my heels into Bane's flanks and rode on ahead.

# *Ten*

King Mark received me with open joy. I knelt at his feet, but he raised me up and embraced me – I could look over his head.

He said, 'You're a man now. How quickly time goes! How long is it since you went away?'

'Three years, lord,' I said. 'I would not have come back, but I heard the news of King Arthur.'

'Ah yes,' said Mark. 'King Arthur, brought low by that traitor . . . Why is nobility always vanquished by slaves?'

'What has happened to Modred?'

We were in the king's room. It was evening. His body-guard sat drinking near at hand, and the tables were filled with a noisy crowd of nobles. It was difficult to talk, especially with his chief advisors, Van and Segward, straining to catch every syllable of our conversation.

Mark had been gazing in front of him in silence, then suddenly, in a loud voice, he said, 'Leave us!'

They stared at him. Segward and Van looked surprised, even indignant.

'You heard what I said,' Mark repeated, conviction growing in his voice, 'leave us.'

One by one, grumbling, they shuffled slowly out. The two slaves hesitated by the door.

'I'll call if I need you. Pull the hanging across. Hurry!'

When we were alone, he got up, went across to the hearth, knelt down and began to stir the fire. 'Are you cold?'

'No, lord.'

He put on a couple of small logs, carefully, like a joiner aligning pieces of wood. He poured more wine into his own glass and refilled mine, and sighed deeply. He said, 'Your coming is the answer to a prayer, Drustan.' He glanced behind him, as if still afraid of being overheard, and then laughed at his stealth. 'My nobles are not what one might call trustworthy.'

I thought of Segward's eyes near-set in his lean, sallow face, of Van's crafty look, not quite concealed by the glistening fat of his childlike cheeks.

'I suppose . . .' I began carefully, '. . . a king can really trust no one.' But as I said this, I thought of Cerridwen, and the memory stopped me short with pain.

When I could once again pay attention, Mark was talking about philosophy . . . 'You don't know how much I've wished I could go to the druids, that's why I took your part against your father, which I shouldn't have done. Of course, for me it was impossible. There was no other heir, or I might have persuaded Cador my father to set me free. But I couldn't. He knew some Latin, and taught me himself . . . I suppose you don't know any Greek, do you?'

'The alphabet, a few words.'

He sighed. 'If only one had books, the freedom to travel – ' He pulled himself up and looked ashamed. 'You must forgive me for talking to you like this, Drustan, but there are so few people here one really has anything in common with. Now, you must play to me. Do you know the "Lament for Geraint, son of Erbin"?'

'Of course,' I said. I played the introduction rather clumsily, because I was thinking of something else, and then began.

> Before Geraint, the enemy of oppression,
> I saw white horses, stained with blood,
> And after the shout a terrible resistance.

> Before Geraint, the enemy of tyranny,
> I saw horses, white with foam,
> And after the shout a terrible torrent.

In Llongborth I saw the rage of slaughter
And biers beyond number
And men bloodstained from the assault of Geraint.

In Llongborth I saw the spurs
Of men who did not flinch through fear of spears
Nor hesitate in draining wine from bright glasses. . . .

One could go on and on. It seemed a strange choice of
song for a king like Mark. 'You've a good voice,' he said.
I nodded. 'You know the song, lord?'
'Yes. I play myself, only a little, I'm afraid. It wouldn't
be fitting.'
He had a sweet speaking voice, without the harsh edge
which often mars mine. I was about to offer him my harp –
it was Cerridwen's, I'd brought it from Kanoel; after all,
I'd had nothing else from her – but Mark sounded wistful,
as if he were afraid he had unbent to me too far. He with-
drew and stood by the window. He seemed about to call
his followers back.
I said, 'Lord, you were going to tell me about Modred.'
This roused him from his new mood and he turned and
smiled at me.
'Lancelin came back, shortly after the battle of Camlon.
Modred was terrified. He thought Lancelin had come to
take possession of Arthur's lands.'
'Hadn't he?'
'No. I must admit from my own point of view I rather
hoped that he might. I'd sooner have Lancelin than
Modred for a neighbour any day. But he had come back
to see the queen. You knew of course that he was her
lover?'
I nodded woodenly.
'His mission was to persuade her to return to Armorica
with him. But she's joined a Christian community at
Treames. She wouldn't agree.'
'Not agree?' For some reason this struck terror into me.
'Why not? Surely, all her life —'
'Her thoughts appear to be of heaven now,' Mark said.

'Neither she nor Lancelin is still young. He too decided to renounce the world. He went back alone to a monastery in Armorica.'

'What a waste!' I said.

Mark raised his eyebrows. 'You're very sure.'

I didn't want to offend him, for it had occurred to me that he too might be baptised. I said, 'So Modred's still king?'

'Yes, but our troubles come from a different source.'

'You mean Erin?'

'Just so.'

'The same thing's happening in Leones. Bands of pirates, coming ashore, killing, raping and stealing whatever they can lay their hands on.'

His face changed, as an adult's does when attending to the woes of a child. 'Cynmor doesn't know how lucky he is. Leones has rocky coasts, hardly a single open harbour; whereas Kernow, especially in the south . . .' He broke off, looking at me anxiously. 'Would you like more wine? Are you tired after your journey? I've been talking a lot. Perhaps you'd prefer to sleep now. We can talk again to-morrow.'

Such delicacy in the consideration of other people's feelings was alien to me. I said, somewhat brusquely, 'Go on, I'm listening.'

Mark hesitated a little, then continued. 'I've been king, Drustan, since I was fourteen. I'm now two-and-thirty. But I remember, even in my father's time, a great many people from Erin came here to settle; boatloads of them, some peaceful and some not so peaceful. When Cador my father said there was no more land for them they took it with the sword. Was this the same in Leones?'

'Not so bad,' I said, 'the coast discouraged them. But there's more and more people from Erin coming to the kingdoms of Powys.'

'And to Alba, too,' he said, 'so I hear through spies.'

There was a pause while he drank and I wondered what was coming. I had lost all sense of awe in being spoken to thus intimately by a great king. I had felt more awe of

62

Cynmor, even of Cerridwen. Mark had little of their majesty; though as I watched him, sitting with his elbows resting on his knees, chin propped in his hands, the firelight flickering on his hair, I thought that here was the heir to Arthur's nobility, if not to his strong right hand.

'Since my grandfather's time,' Mark said, 'Kernow has owed a tribute to the king of Laighin. Laighin is the south-easternmost kingdom of Erin, whose coastline is nearest to Kernow. Every three years we must send them a slave ship, full of young men and girls. Since I became king I've refused to send the ship. Now, at last, the King of Laighin is growing angry. He's being worsted at home by the King of Mumha, so I'm informed, and needs all the prestige he can get. The last ambassador, who came a month ago, threatened me with invasion . . . Drustan, I'm at my wit's end.'

'But surely if his own borders are being attacked, the King of Laighin can't afford to send his troops here?'

'Ah, the King of Mumha would become his ally then. There's nothing these people like better, except perhaps cattle raiding. It's impossible for them to live in peace.'

I frowned and waited. 'My father would put all his troops at your disposal, of course,' I said.

Mark smiled bitterly. 'Segward and Van want me to send the ship, so they can make sure it's loaded up with all the people *they* dislike. Sometimes, I despair . . .' He broke off.

I got up and put away my harp in its soft leather bag. As I was drawing up the cord round the neck, Mark said, 'It would please me if you could stay here a while.'

'I want to stay, if I can be useful, lord; at least until next spring. Then . . .' My life stretched before me, bleak and uninviting as a mountain road.

'Stay,' said Mark. Then, hesitating, he added, 'One more thing, I'd like to ask you, if I may.'

'Of course.' I began to tremble. I wondered for a dreadful moment if some rumour about Cerridwen had reached Castle Dor.

'Are you a Christian?'

I was so relieved that my 'No!' came out more light-heartedly than I had meant.

Mark tried not to betray his disappointment. 'I've been one for a year,' he said. 'My sister, your mother, was a Christian, you know, one of the very first. She and our mother were baptised by Piran, the first monk to come here from Erin. I wonder she never persuaded your father to adopt the faith.'

'They had been married less than a year when she died,' I said. It seemed strange, saying it quite calmly. I had never been able to discuss her with anyone before. 'Do you remember her?' I asked him.

Sadly, he shook his head. 'We were near in age, but she was kept close. She was beautiful, with fair hair. You're not very like her. Perhaps the mouth, or the eyes, but only if you look gentle. When you're fierce you're all Cynmor's child.'

I blushed, for I was not used to having my face examined. He smiled when he saw it, and I felt after all the space of years between us.

'Your mother would have liked you to be baptised,' he said.

'I've never heard anything of the Christian teaching,' I said.

'How I wish you'd been here last summer,' Mark went on. 'A monk named Paul Aurelian passed through my kingdom. We were holding the Midsummer Festival when he arrived. There were horse races, and the people had decorated the trees and bushes. They were dancing round the standing stones out on the moor. I was dancing too —' He broke off. 'Paul preached to us there and then. The people stopped their dancing and fell silent. How he terrified us! Afterwards he baptised two score in the river. I stripped down to my under-tunic and went in along with the rest.'

'What did he say?' I wondered what spell this Christian had used to make so many people do his will.

'If I could tell you that,' Mark said, 'I'd leave Kernow tomorrow for a life of travelling and preaching. But how

64

can I? He talked quite simply, but with great understanding, about our life here on earth with its trials, disappointments and pain. Then he spoke about our life in heaven where we are one with god. As he spoke I seemed to see things clearly for the first time. But Drustan, no heaven awaits those who are unbaptised. They go to hell, where slow fires roast them day and night for ever.'

His words sent a chill up my spine. In so far as the druids had committed themselves to the possibility of an after life, they taught the doctrine of the transmigration of souls. 'How do you know that this heaven and this hell exist?' I asked.

'I've experienced them in myself,' Mark said. 'I know.'

This seemed to me no answer, but I didn't say so. 'I'd like to meet this man,' I said.

'He's gone to Gaul now. Perhaps you should go out and seek baptism, Drustan. I'll pray for you.'

He spoke as if he were doing me a special favour, like bestowing a heavy bracelet or a glass cup. Then he began giving me presents in earnest, so I thanked him and protested that gifts were for leave-taking, not arrival.

'I hope I've not been tedious, Drustan. You're not weary, are you?'

In fact by this time I was so weary that it took all my will to prevent my eyelids falling shut. 'No, lord,' I said. 'It's been an honour to speak with you for so long.'

As I passed through the outer room I saw that his followers eyed me suspiciously: I was someone to be reckoned with. I slipped naked between soft blankets on a bed in the corner of the king's room, and lay awake, marvelling at myself. For once even the thought of Cerridwen brought me a sense of victory and not defeat.

# *Eleven*

I was quickly established as King Mark's new favourite. I sat by him at meals and at Council. I went riding with him, played draughts with him, sang to him. I slept in his bedroom, from which I learned since his baptism all women had been banished. I even accompanied him sometimes to his Christian services in the tiny chapel that had been built at Castle Dor, but I never felt the least desire to be baptised myself. I was careful to remain my own man. My daily practice bouts with Gorvenal continued, but now I could beat him almost every time. I kept up my music too, and spent so much time alone working out songs that Mark, half teasing, accused me of having taken up with some girl. I let him think what he liked. It was a useful defence against the wagging tongues that maintained I shared his bed.

This wasn't the only scandal that Van and Segward assiduously spread. They claimed that when I played to the king I was putting a druid's spell on him, and my wicked intention was to be made his heir. They even raked up the story that I had stolen my horse from King Maelgwn of Gwynedd, though I had taken to calling him simply 'Bane'. But they didn't dare say these things to my face. I was a bard. I could wield the deadliest weapon of all: satire. By means of satire a poet could cause warts to appear on his enemy's face, prevent his cows from giving milk, even cause his death. For doesn't the ancient *Triad* say, 'It is death to mock a poet'?

I would never have stood all this in the ordinary way, but for one thing, I grew fond of Mark. He was a man one could not help but love. Like Hywel, his nature was sweet and open, and sometimes he made me ashamed of my own deviousness and dark thoughts. His mind too was as quick as any I had encountered outside Môn, and his poetry, when at last I prevailed on him to recite to me, was cleverly made, and beautiful. I thought, I'll stay till spring, it's the least I can do. Then I'll move on, perhaps to Gaul; perhaps the devastation there is not as great as one hears.

Just when we thought the weather had broken and winter come, the ship arrived. She was a fine ship, with a delicately carved figurehead and painted sails. The ambassadors who came ashore were richly dressed. They had brought Mark a message from King Angus of Laighin. The message was this.

'The three-yearly tribute from Kernow to Laighin is long overdue. King Angus, a wise man and a Christian king, is accordingly willing to strike a bargain with King Mark. He offers King Mark the chance of paying off his debt with one stroke. On this fair ship King Angus has sent a mighty champion, the Morholt, his own wife's brother. King Mark must find a champion of his own, daring enough to meet the Morholt in single combat. If King Mark's champion can slay the Morholt, Kernow's debt to Laighin will be paid. If Laighin's champion has the victory, King Mark must send two tribute ships of slaves, instead of one.'

The crowd began to murmur, and I felt a vague disquiet. Turning, I caught Segward's near-set eyes on me. Van plucked at his sleeve and whispered a few words in his ear. Then again they turned towards me, and the look in their eyes was that of hungry men licking their lips over a carcass of meat that the cook is turning on the spit. With one accord they began to speak to King Mark. I was too far away to hear what was said, but I saw Mark's hands tighten on the arms of his chair, and as they talked on he gripped harder, so that the knuckles showed white.

Surely, I thought, panic-stricken, surely . . . There must be someone else.

Segard and Van, who had hated me from the first evening I came back to Castle Dor, made sure that there was no one else.

'I must speak to him,' Mark said, loud enough for me to hear it. He beckoned me over. This was one Council where I hadn't sat by his side. He didn't meet my eyes, and he spoke so low that I had to bend my head to catch his words. 'Drustan, they want *you* to fight him . . .' I nodded and said nothing. I was too proud to ask him if he couldn't find another champion. 'The Morholt is the queen's brother. We must find a combatant of equally noble blood. You're a king's son . . . You know, don't you, that if I had an heir I'd have to send him?'

I nodded. It was true. Mark had no choice. But it maddened me to have been sacrified by Van and Segward.

'How old is Morholt?' I said.

The fight was to take place next day. I spent the evening with Gorvenal. He rubbed me down with oil. I had missed my bout that day, but it couldn't be helped. Now it would only tire me. Gorvenal had slipped down to the ship and hung about, picking up all the information he could find. The Morholt was in the flower of his strength, a devil with a sword, he had no equal in no-holds-barred wrestling.

I lay on my stomach naked before the blazing fire while Gorvenal's strong fingers kneaded my shoulder and back muscles. He was talking. 'He's ten years older than you, he's twice as tough. He's killed more men than you've had hot suppers; yes, and laid more women too by the looks of him. Your one hope is to use your wits. Surprise him, if you can.'

I pillowed my cheek on my arm and thought of Myrddin . . . my father . . . Cerridwen . . . Gorvenal's hands began on the backs of my thighs.

If I didn't run away, by this time tomorrow I would certainly be dead.

We were to fight on a tiny island at the mouth of the river, near the place where I had sat with Myrddin that first day. Each of us rowed out to the island in his own boat. Morholt managed his oars skilfully, and though I had spent the summer rowing in the bays round Kanoel, he reached the island before I did. I followed him at a steady pace, trying not to get too winded before we even touched swords.

He drew his rowing boat up on the beach, and stood, hands on hips, waiting for me to come. He wore heavy armour, cunningly made of interlocking rings. As I reached the shallows he drew his sword impatiently and brandished it in the air. From far away I heard the crowds lining the edge of the shore give a thin cheer.

He was a great bull of a man, not so tall as I, but powerfully built, with massive shoulders and legs. I pulled my boat up on the beach and walked towards him. Strangely, I felt as I had when Cerridwen stood naked in the orchard. I felt the same awe and lust and fear. Seeing me, he threw back his head and laughed out loud. I caught a glimpse of white teeth and red hair flowing from under his leather helmet.

*Morholt!* The name came back to me like a blow. Surely it was Morholt that Brendan mentioned after our first fight on the cliffs of Môn. This was his brother.

The sword was already moving, Morholt didn't want me to have time to recover my breath. But I wasn't playing that game. I made him an ironical bow. 'By your leave,' I said. 'There's a matter I must attend to first.'

I went down to the water, and shoved his boat off. It bobbed away quite fast with the ebbing tide.

'Hey!' he shouted. 'What d'you think you're doing?'

'See for yourself. It stands to reason only one of us will be able to row back. *If* it's you, you can take my boat.'

He pushed back the useless helmet and scratched his head. I felt hope warming me for the first time since Mark's shy voice condemned me to death. The Morholt's *stupid*! I thought exultantly.

This island was sandy, with a few boulders dotted over the ridge in the centre part. There was a stunted tree with twisted roots dug into the sand like clawing fingers. I must get him to the middle, I thought, then I may stand a chance. But I was powerless. We circled round parrying each other's strokes like two professionals in a show bout, careful not to do any damage because it's their living. It was like a dance. My breath came faster, and I could feel the sweat prickling down the back of my tunic under my armour. My sword arm shook.

Then, more quickly than I had thought him capable of,

Morholt parried a stroke of mine, got through my guard, and gave me a cut in the shoulder, not deep, but painful. The blood came fast.

Once more we circled endlessly, panting. His lips drew back in a half-grin, half-snarl, his teeth bared in concentration. When I thought I had lulled him enough I tried a feint. I pretended to slip on the rough ground and half stumbled. He was on me in a moment. He was quick for his size. I only just turned out of reach in time, and managed to strike him a glancing blow on the thigh; but as luck had it, my sword caught the rim of his shield, and his grasp was weakened for a moment by the pain. The shield fell to the beach with a thud.

I seized my opportunity, and closed in with overhead slashes, a stroke I favour because my extra height gives me the advantage; but he was ready for me. I'd hoped to finish him quickly, but my onslaught soon turned to defence. I began to give ground, backing towards the tree in the middle of the island. Blood dripped from my elbow.

Morholt was closer now. With all my strength I jabbed my shield at him. It caught him in the guts and he went down with a surprised grunt. The bright red hair was dimmed with sand. But I couldn't get near enough to use my sword. He kept me at bay, kicking out with his legs. I couldn't risk throwing at him, for if I missed I'd be unarmed.

I felt panic rising in me. I'd used all the tricks I knew. As I hesitated, he scooped up sand on his sword point and flung it in my face. Then, as he grabbed my ankles, I knew I had underestimated him. He was not stupid, only careful. I was reckless and now he had my measure.

He was on me. I felt his hands go round my neck in a stranglehold. I thrashed about under him, panic-stricken as a virgin, and as ineffectual. But I felt his legs part, and crashed my knee up into his groin. The fingers loosened and I twisted sideways out from under him.

I could see again and quickly looked for my sword. As it happened, both our swords were lying together, a little way from the tree, as if we had placed them carefully side by side. I started forward, but he caught me again with a foot behind my heel and his other foot against my opposite knee. I toppled backwards like a felled tree, and I thought, I deserve to be dead.

I fell with my head in the water. It was this that saved me, for the shock sobered me, and I was able once more to plan as he came at me. I got on top and held his face under the water. Long slow moments passed as I held him, and then, gradually, with a sick fear, I realised that he was the stronger. Little by little he was pushing me from him. Little by little he was heaving himself up, as a drowned corpse is lifted by the invincible current. The breath sobbed in my throat and my shoulders were shaking. I was almost exhausted. I felt his strength, the strength of seasoned oak, and knew that he had not yet begun to tire. His face came up out of the water and he took a deep gasping breath. Soon he would turn me over and hold me down till I was dead.

My instinct to lunge back for the swords had been right. I saw them still in my mind's eye lying so near, together by the tree.

As fast as my exhausted limbs would serve, I released my hold, slithered from his grasp and dived towards the tree. I heard the suck and splash of the sea as he came after me. My hand grasped my sword hilt and I stood up and with all my remaining strength smashed the blade at his skull. But even as I saw it cleave deeply, white as bone and then red as blood, I felt an answering fire in my side and fell to the sand beside him.

I was drowning in a sea of blood. I had embraced Cerridwen, but her breasts had pierced my ribs like a sword. I felt Mark's tears on my closed eyelids, heard him calling me and tried to answer, but I could not swim up and touch his hand.

Time passed, but I lay suspended in time. Often I saw the faces of Mark and Gorvenal, and tried to speak to them. Sometimes doctors came. A fire blazed and snow fell. The pain of my wound never left me, and by the time I returned to the world of men, the pain had changed me.

Mark visited me and we talked as before, but my heart was hardened against him. He could walk and run and ride in the fresh air, while I had to lie still indoors, rotting to death. Sometimes when I was in bad pain, or feverish, I had to ask him to leave me. He used to try to sit by me, to stroke my forehead and pray. I could have fastened my teeth in his hand like a bad-tempered dog.

Spring came, and with it came despair. My wound was poisoned. It would not heal. I knew I'd never leave that room until I was carried out, a corpse. One night the fever returned and I thought I was in hell. I was being borne across the fiery lake in a ship with black sails. Next day I was much weaker and Mark told me he had sent for my father. Cynmor came and I held his hand and begged him to bless me.

'Drustan, don't despair,' he said. 'Can you understand? Cerridwen has come with me. She wants to talk to you alone. Do you consent?'

I nodded. When she entered I saw that she was pregnant. Her face changed as she came towards me. Cynmor closed the hangings. She sat on the stool by my bed and took my hands, hers were as cold as ice.

'Have you your poison cup now?' I muttered, 'I'd drink it gladly.'

'I wanted to come before,' she said, 'but your father was unwilling and I couldn't insist. But this time —' She broke off. 'Drustan, you must trust me.'

I laughed.

'I think I can cure you. That is, if you want to live.'

'Of course,' I said, 'if I could be a man again and not a rotting corpse.'

'Then listen. The Queen of Laighin is a witch. Her name is Deirdre. The Morholt was her brother. Deirdre must have put some spell on Morholt's sword, and painted it with poison. That's why your wound won't heal. Unless you can secure the antidote it never will.'

'Let Mark go to Laighin and steal it for me,' I said. 'He owes me a favour.'

'Besides,' she went on, ignoring me, 'Queen Deirdre and

73

her lady, Branwen, are skilled physicians. If anyone can cure you, they can.'

'How do you know so much?' I asked, cursing, for my speech was slurring and the sweat ran down my chest.

'Branwen is a friend of mine. She used to visit me on the Islands of the Dead, before I married your father . . . Now, tell me, will you go to Laighin?'

'D'you think I'm mad?' I said. 'I killed Queen Deirdre's brother.'

'How will she know *you* killed him? Choose a different name and lie about your kindred.'

'I'll be recognised.'

'*Recognised?* Even I hardly knew you. Haven't you seen yourself lately, Drustan?'

I knew that my bones showed sharply through my skin, but I wasn't prepared for the face she showed me in the king's mirror: the eyes, sunk deep into hollow sockets, burnt brightly with sickness, and the cheekbones seemed almost to pierce the pallid flesh.

As I winced she smiled and took away the mirror.

I said. 'Cerridwen, do you still hate me? Are you still trying to encompass my death?'

'No,' she said. 'I've done what you told me. You told me to love Cynmor. I'm bearing him another child, which was what he wanted.'

'And how,' I asked with a sneer, 'can you be sure it's his child you're bearing?'

'Spare me, Drustan,' she said. 'Since that day I've had no man but your father. And I do love him, believe me.'

I couldn't hate her, and I was too sick to desire her. 'I've always remembered how beautiful you seemed in the orchard,' I said. 'But you weren't for me.'

'No,' she said. 'I know that now. I knew it then, but I thought I could bend fate to my will. But it's stronger than any of us, stronger than all our wills.'

'Cerridwen,' I said, 'can you see? Will I be cured of this wound in Erin?'

'There are more wounds than one,' she said, and kissed me before she went away.

74

# Twelve

My consciousness returned.

I was lying flat on my back on a bed. In my first terror I thought that my hands were tied, but then I realised I was a prisoner of my own weakness. My last memory was of the ship. The sailors must have brought me to land; but where they had left me I had no idea.

All that was within my view was a ceiling, low and rough, of wood. I turned my head carefully and saw a small window with a blind of plaited reeds drawn down. The wall was bare, but for a crude carving about as high as a man; a small cross-piece was nailed to a wooden upright, and a circle enclosed the join. Birds and animals chased each other round the cross, or sat lop-sidedly still.

I closed my eyes, turned my head, and waited for the banging inside my skull to cease before I opened them again. On this side I saw a door, a low bench, and a strip of bare beaten-earth floor. This was no king's house, I thought.

I closed my eyes again. I felt peaceful, almost ready to sleep. I could hear faint chanting from quite close at hand. I tried to remember where I had heard the like before, and could not, but was lulled all the same. Then the door opened and a middle-aged woman came in.

She was dressed in a long full robe of unbleached wool with a hood over her head. A scarf was tied tightly round her face, hiding her hair. She came up to the bed and bent over me, feeling with her fingers for my wrist. I opened my eyes and we looked at each other for some moments, then she tucked the blanket over me and said, 'So you're awake at last?'

'Are you the queen?'

She laughed, showing white, even teeth. Her mouth was firm and straight. There was no paint on her face. 'I am Angharad, abbess of this house,' she said.

My peace was broken. I struggled to sit up. 'But I was to be taken to Queen Deirdre!'

'Hush.' She pressed against my shoulder, pushing me back on to the bed. She was strong for a woman and I was as weak as a child. 'You are in the monastery at Taghmon. Don't fret yourself. We found you outside the gates. At first we thought you'd been left for us to bury.'

'How long have I been here?'

'Almost a month. Tell me who you are, and what kindred you come from. Are you a Christian?'

I shook my head. 'My name's Kai. I'm kindred to King Arthur.'

'When you are stronger,' she said, 'we will talk of this. Have you never heard tell of Christ the son of god?'

'No,' I said. I was tiring and tried desperately to marshal my thoughts into some kind of plan that would get me to the queen.

She hesitated and then turned back to me. 'Earthly life is vain,' she said. 'It's useless to strive for it, or for riches. I am abbess of three score monks and a score of nuns at Taghmon. All these souls have dedicated themselves to serving Christ. In these times of slaughter and despair, Christ is the only certainty. Your wife may be kidnapped by barbarians, your lands looted, your wealth stolen. Your children may die of the plague. But if you live in Christ no earthly ill can hurt you. Death itself loses all terror. You are yourself close to death. Think of these things.' She rose to go.

'*No!*' I dragged myself up, gasping at the pain in my side. 'If I stay here I *will* die, but the queen can cure me. A witch told me that Queen Deirdre knows magic skills of healing. I've had this wound half a year. Only magic can save me now.'

Her face grew stern. 'Miserable man,' she said, 'if you die unbaptised it doesn't matter a jot whether you die today or in a hundred years. The pain you feel now is nothing to the tortures of the damned.'

'I care nothing for any god,' I said, 'but if you keep me here against my will, then this Christ you speak of is a god without mercy.'

I was finished, and lay back against the pillow gasping for breath. Angharad gazed at me thoughtfully. 'The men that abandoned you left by your side a sword and a harp . . . Are you a bard?'

I nodded. She spat on the floor. 'A curse on the druids! Not content with sacrificing children to their monstrous gods, they lead pure souls astray into the paths of evil.' I lay quiet. At length she said, 'Very well, I can baptise no one against his will. If you must go to the queen, then you must. She may be a witch, but King Angus and their daughter are Christians, praise god. Perhaps you will listen to them. Sleep now . . .'

After that she visited me for a short while each day, and sometimes read to me from a book she called the Bible. I had never met a woman of such authority and learning. I asked her once if it was a common thing among Christians to place women in charge of men. 'No,' she said. 'In all Erin there is only Brigid, Hilda and myself. But your question betrays how little you know of our teaching. In Christ there is no male and no female. All souls are equal, the man and the woman, the king and the slave.'

The Christians take a vow of chastity when they retreat from the world; even husbands and wives live apart.

The food was very meagre, though I did not observe fasts, as Angharad did. A monk looked after me, fed and cleaned me, but he never spoke, and when I asked the abbess, she told me that he had taken a vow of a year's silence.

'What's your mortification?' I asked.

She shook her head. 'We do not boast of our self denials,' she said.

At last Angharad told me that she had arranged for me to be taken to the queen.

77

'Her daughter comes here often. I'm teaching her to read and write Latin, and we say prayers together. Tomorrow she will bring extra slaves with her, and a cart for you to ride in. It isn't very far.'

However short the journey was, it was certain to be painful for me. I wished that I could beg for some potion or other to make me sleep, but these Christians seemed to use no medicines, eschewing them, I suppose, as magic. Certainly they had given none to me. They seemed to think that pain, in itself, had some special efficacy, and that the flesh was so evil that unless constantly tormented, it was bound to sin.

'Think of Christ who suffered on the cross for our sins,' Angharad said. 'However long your journey is, it will seem but a moment compared to that eternity.'

It was long enough.

While the princess was with Angharad, two of her servants came, heaved me on to a litter, and carried me to the cart that stood in the sunlight in the yard of the monastery. I lay and looked at the canvas roof and sides that flapped a little in the breeze, and thought, now that I was on my way to the queen, how it might have been better after all to have stayed at Taghmon; for there, even if I wasn't healed, at least I was still alive, whereas if Queen Deirdre recognised me as the killer of her brother, my life wouldn't be worth a pin.

Then I heard voices, Angharad's low and measured, and the soft tones of a young girl.

'I will *try*,' the girl was saying, rather wistfully it seemed. 'but I'm not sure I'm ready yet.'

'But, child,' Angharad said, 'think of your soul. The end of the world is at hand. It will come within our lifetimes, make no mistake. Do you want to be condemned to everlasting fire simply for a whim? *Make* yourself ready, before it's too late.'

'Yes . . .' said the girl unhappily. 'Sometimes I feel such a terrible sense of foreboding, of sin! Oh Angharad, pray for me, pray for me! If only I had your faith.'

'Keep your tears for god, child, not for me. Now you

must go. The sick man is in the cart. Don't let the driver go too fast; it might kill him, and he's unbaptised.'

'Unbaptised! Is he a young man?'

'Old – young . . . He has suffered.'

'Then I won't delay. If anyone can help him, mother can. Slave, fetch my horse!'

It was certainly the queen's daughter; there was no humility in that command. There were farewells, which were lost to me, then horses' hooves clip-clopping on the beaten earth of the yard, and the cart began to move, swaying steadily. I gripped my sword hilt with one hand, the frame of my harp with the other, gritted my teeth, and felt the first pain run through my side.

I remember little of my arrival at Dun Ailinne. Once again there are only cloudy memories, a glimpse of faces, and a lock of bronze-coloured hair burning in my mind's eye. Then, suddenly it seemed, I was awake, propped up on pillows, and able to grasp what was happening around me. My first reaction was panic, for they had shaved my beard. But I seemed to be among friends.

I was in a small room, paved with stone flags, and with smoothed stone walls. There was a fire burning in the hearth and a pot hung over it from a hook in the chimney-piece. A woman was stirring the contents of the pot. She wore a dark red dress with gold on the hem, and red hair hung in long plaits past her waist. Her back was towards me. As I watched her, she added a pinch of something to the pot from a jar that stood on a shelf close by, turned, and finding me watching her, said, 'Awake? About time too.'

Her hair was bound with a red gauze veil. Her face was the strangest I ever saw, with high prominent cheekbones and a narrow chin. Her nose was long and her eyes deep set; at first I thought, how ugly she is! Then she smiled at me, and I didn't think her ugly at all. She was in her middle years, but still slender. This was the queen.

'Tell me,' she said briskly, 'which of my kin gave you that wound?'

79

'I don't know,' I said. 'I was wounded at the battle of Camlon.'

'Camlon, you say? There were none of my kin with Arthur, or against him for that matter.' She gave a short laugh. 'It doesn't matter if you choose to lie to me, I will try to heal you. I'm the only one who can, you know. I make the poison and I make the antidote. You were wise to come here.' She shot a look at me. 'Angharad says you're not a Christian.'

'No, I'm not.'

'Good, I wouldn't heal you if you were. Well —'

She went over to the pot, unhooked it, stood it on a small table by the hearth, and began to dip cloths into the boiling liquid. A faint aromatic smell reached my nostrils. The queen wrung out the cloths and came over to the couch where I was lying. She pulled down the blankets that covered my naked body and clapped the poultice to my festering side. It was so hot I let out a yell. She held my shoulders with one hand, and kept the cloths in place with the other. I ground my teeth.

'At least,' said the queen, 'you can't be the man who killed my brother Morholt.' She took my indrawn breath for pain not fear and held the poultice more firmly in place. 'Because the man who killed the Morholt is dead. Those bungling ambassadors swore to it before the chariots pulled them apart. If not I wouldn't have slept till I'd avenged him! But that's past . . . Morholt's dead . . . All the talk in the world won't bring him back, nor all the magic.' She laughed into my face. The sweat was dripping off my chin. 'Poor Angus, trying to comfort me with his talk about heaven. As if Morholt could go to a Christian heaven; he was unbaptised and a lecher. There are five of his bastards here at Dun Ailinne.'

She stopped talking, lifted off the poultice and tossed the cloths into the fire. Then she bound on a bandage of fresh linen, passing the strips round my shoulders and back to hold the pad firmly in place. I was feeling sick.

'You may be a liar,' Deirdre said, 'but you're a brave

80

man. I've had old soldiers beg with tears to have one of my poultices taken off.'

'I want it to heal,' I said.

Heal the wound did.

I submitted to the queen's torture twice a day, and slowly the pus drained away, the edges of the wound closed and the flesh grew firm. I could walk round holding on to her shoulders, and as Midsummer drew near, I was well enough to be impatient to be out and about. I began to think that it would be wise to make good my escape while my true identity was still unguessed. Who knew when Brendan might return? I had put on flesh, he might recognise me. But I lingered for many reasons.

I was fascinated by the people of Dun Ailinne. I had never before been in a land that the Romans had not conquered. Even the druids of Môn had felt the might of Rome, but to these people it was no more than hearsay. They had gone their own way for countless ages, and their ways were more devious than ours, less of logic and more of poetry. For example, they had no loyalty higher than clan loyalty, and there was no hope of justice outside the might of the clan and its power of vendetta. The people of Britain have at least been welded into some kind of unity by the need to oppose the Saxons, but the people of Erin have never had to face a common enemy, and so the five great kingdoms, Ulaid, Connachta and Midhe in the north, and Mumha and Laighin in the south, are constantly warring for land, and cattle raiding is a favourite sport. Even the coming of Christianity seems to have done nothing to settle the feuding.

Thus much knowledge I gained from careful questioning of the queen, who would always talk freely on any subject. Though not so learned as Angharad, Deirdre was just as remarkable, and her dry sense of humour was more to my taste than the abbess's sermonising.

Deirdre had a maid who would sometimes come to attend to me if the queen was too busy. This maid was a small, dark creature, as silent as the queen was talkative. This was Branwen, who had been Cerridwen's friend, and

81

my thoughts often turned to her in the endless hours of the long days when I lay half dozing on my bed in the small stone room. And my thoughts also turned to the princess.

I sought her out. One day, having walked farther than usual, I ventured into the queen's rooms, and found the princess sitting among her ladies. They were a diligent little circle, busily spinning and sewing, but the princess's head was turned towards the window and her work hung from her idle fingers. She sighed. The sun, shining through her hair, made it seem on fire.

I dropped my stick, and she started up with a cry of fear.

'Lady Essylt!'

It was Branwen who admonished her. The princess drew a deep breath.

'What is the meaning of this intrusion?' she said, but her voice wasn't quite steady. I suppose she was about fifteen.

'I have come to thank you,' I said. 'You saved me from death. I am the man you brought from the house at Taghmon, and the queen has healed my wound.'

She was no higher than my breast, and her white dress made her look like a child, but gold was heavy round her neck, her waist, her fingers.

She said, 'I'm glad you're well again!'

I said, 'May I rest here a little?'

She hesitated and then said, 'Yes, of course. Branwen, fetch some wine.' Her hands fluttered at her breast, her hair, and came to rest like butterflies in her lap.

I longed to reassure her, to tell her not to fear me, and promise that I meant her no ill. I would have liked to do her some service, as a tribute to her beauty and innocence; but Branwen handed me the wine with a venomous look, so when I had drunk it I bowed and took my leave.

'Lady Essylt,' I said, 'I am in your debt. I hope one day I will repay you.'

'I shall remember,' she said.

I still had not encountered King Angus. By all accounts he was a mild-mannered man, much harried by the queen and her bellicose male relatives. After this meeting with

Princess Essylt, I did not venture so far again, but sat in the sun in the yard outside my own doorway. I could feel the strength coming back into my body.

Queen Deirdre still looked in to see me briefly each evening just before supper, to exchange a few words and rub sweet-smelling ointment into my side. One evening soon after my first exchange with Essylt, she had me strip and kneaded my muscles with her nobbly fingers. She used oil but it hurt a good deal.

She asked suddenly, 'What is your interest in the princess?'

I reached across her for my tunic, but she slapped away my hands. 'Not so fast. I'd as soon talk to you like that. Branwen tells me that you wandered into her rooms the other day. What are you after?'

'Nothing,' I said. 'I wanted to thank the princess.'

'Have you a wife?' asked the queen.

'No,' I said, before I had time to consider that a lie might be safer.

'But you're fond of girls?'

'Well, naturally, I —'

'Do you prefer them young or old, whores or virgins?' She went on to enquire more closely about my tastes. How could I tell her that I'd never had a girl? I was sweating with fear. I managed to mutter, 'I'm chaste.'

She raised her eyebrows. 'Are you indeed? Well, then, you're wasting yourself! But listen, do you find my daughter beautiful?'

'Very.'

'And modest?'

'Yes.'

'I want you to give her music lessons.'

'But I —'

'Keep quiet! I must find something to take her thoughts from prayers and fasting and the penances that Angharad gives her. She's trying to persuade her to renounce the world, to waste her life in that stinking religious house at Taghmon . . .'

I thought of the harsh discipline, of the princess's

delicate body broken by the menial work she would be forced to perform, her health damaged by cold and fasting. '. . . Don't let her go to Taghmon!'

'You're on my side, then. Good! Get dressed.' I complied. 'I may tell you, I've received an offer of marriage for her, from no less a person than Cormac mac Dairmait, the son of the High King of Tara.' I buckled my belt. 'Think,' said the queen, 'of the fine sons she would bear if Cormac bedded her.'

I turned away to hide my face. It angered me to think of the princess becoming a nun, but that she would be the helpless victim of lust and childbirth seemed to me an even worse fate.

I knew it was dangerous for me to stay, that I must leave forthwith; and yet I did not. Instead I began teaching the princess to play the harp. She was quick to learn, and I loved the peaceful afternoons I spent with her, while the rain fell softly outside, and her little fingers tried to match mine on the strings of her fine harp, inlaid with mother-of-pearl.

In return she told me something about the history of her people, and how they were first called the Milesians, after the three sons of Mileadh, King of Hispania. These sons, Heremon, Heber and Ir, came to Erin and conquered the land from its previous inhabitants, the race of the Danaans. The Danaans were very beautiful and semi-divine. 'Even now,' Essylt said, 'there are some left in Erin; but if a mortal woman marries one of them, or if a hero marries a fairy lady, then they are taken away to the Land of Youth, where the Danaans live, and where a whole year seems like a day. So, of course, if a mortal comes back to Erin, he finds his friends all dead, his former home a grass-grown ruin, and himself suddenly an old, old man. Can you imagine it? How terrible! I'm sure I'd stay in the Land of Youth, I'd never risk coming back, would you?'

She told me too some of their old legends: how Maeve, Queen of Connachta, made war against Concobar and his famous Red Branch heroes, of his fort at Emain Macha, and of the deeds of Cú Chulainn, the greatest hero of them all. I knew of these tales from my years on Môn, but I was amazed when the princess told me that scholars in Erin were now writing them down.

'Writing?' I asked. 'What, in Latin?'

'Latin?' she said. 'Oh no, in our language. Can it be that you don't know how to write?'

And so, in return for my lessons, she began teaching me how.

One evening, just as we were parting, she said, 'Do you know what happens in two weeks' time?'

I shook my head. 'Tell me, lady.'

'The *Feis*!' she cried, and all her ladies stopped sewing and clapped their hands, like her, in excitement.

'What's that?' I asked.

'I forget you're a foreigner. It's the Midsummer Feast, a great festival, the *Feis Temrach*. It's held by the High King, Dairmait, at his seat at Tara, and all his kin, the Uí Néill come from the north with their followers . . . And, oh, there's a feast, and ceremonial. It only happens once every three years, and I was a child last time we went. That was six years ago. Father didn't dare take us to the last *Feis*; he'd just been baptised, and there was a war between Laighin and Midhe. Of course it's over now, and mother insists that we shall all go again. Perhaps I shouldn't really go. It's a pagan festival, after all, and I *am* baptised, but it's *so* exciting – will you come?'

There was so much eagerness in her flushed, upturned face that I was disturbed, as if a child had begged me for a sweetmeat and I found myself empty-handed.

'Yes,' I said, 'I'll come . . . If it will please you.'

Then her ladies whirled her away in a crazy dance, holding hands in a circle, stamping with their feet, skipping and turning with their veils streaming, and I went away. I could manage without a stick now, if I went slowly.

# Thirteen

Dun Ailinne was thrown into a turmoil by preparations for the *Feis*. The cooks toiled from dawn to dusk, baking vast loaves of bread in intricate designs, to present, so they told me, to the High King. From this I deduced that whatever strife there had been between King Angus and Dairmait, it was not the former who had emerged with honour. The ladies stitched very busily, making fine clothes for the festival.

I had not arranged to travel with anyone, but in the event it was simple to get a lift. I just stood at the gate until an open cart with a little room in the back trundled by, clung on to the tail-board and heaved myself into the giggling mass of girls. The effort left me panting like a hound, but they thought my exhaustion was feigned and laughed uproariously. I pretended to be drunk and lay back to sleep. The miles jogged by.

It was a very different journey from the previous one, which I thought would be my last if pain could settle the matter. This was a holiday trip. Everyone wore bright colours, red, green and blue, and garlands of flowers, even the Christians. They seemed to forget their gloomy god of pain, they laughed and sang songs along with the rest. A plump girl tossed a garland on to my head and plonked herself on my lap. I laughed and tickled her, and forgot for a moment who I was; and that between my pallet and the wooden bench at Dun Ailinne, there was a harp that had come from the Islands of the Dead, and a chipped sword whose missing piece had lodged in a dead man's skull.

Towards the evening of the second day, our laughing procession toiled up the slope to the mighty hill fort of

Tara, over its three great banks and ditches. Every bush on the hillside was decorated with bright ribbons and small ornaments, and there was a constant movement of people in gay clothes calling greetings to us, and telling us to hurry and be sure not to miss the feast.

Inside the gates it was more like a market place than a fort. Stalls protected from the sun by garish canopies sold ale to drink and bread rolls stuffed with ham. Jewellers displayed cheap trinkets. There was a juggler, and a man who ate burning torches and a fellow with a bear on a chain who made it dance by beating its hind legs with a stick.

I made out the royal party, and went slowly towards them. As I drew near, I could see King Angus, a small fair man, cowering under the wrath of Queen Deirdre, who looked magnificent in scarlet and white.

'What is it?' I asked Branwen, who was lurking, inconspicuous, on the edge of the group.

She raised her eyebrows in surprise at seeing me. 'King Dairmait of Tara has kept no place for us from Dun Ailinne,' she said. 'Queen Deirdre is furious at missing the ceremony.'

'What happens?' I asked.

She covered her mouth with her hand, smiling behind her fingers. 'The High King marries the goddess, he sows his seed in the furrow.' Her eyes mocked me. I moved away.

At some distance, gathered round another fire, I could see King Angus and the queen, still talking, and the Princess Essylt. Beside her sat a dark man I didn't recognise. How humiliated they were! For they were of royal blood, and Angus was over-king of Laighin. But Dairmait had slighted them, because he thought them of no account, petty foes to be anihilated with one hand, weak friends with nothing to offer him in the way of material advantage. Poor little Essylt, I thought with a pang, what'll become of her, female heir to a tottering kingdom? One of her mother's kin will kill her to get her out of the way, or shut her up at Taghmon, or some man will marry her wanting nothing but her rank, and she won't sing like a bird then.

My thoughts were interrupted by Branwen. She slipped

quietly into the place beside me, and gave me a cup of ale. I drained it, and we sat without speaking, staring into the leaping flames of the fire. The fat from the meat dripped down, making the fire sizzle and hiss.

'Drink some more ale,' she said. 'It's not good to be sober at the *Feis Temrach*.'

I nodded and she fetched me another cup. I drank that too; I was beginning to feel less lonely. Her hand stole into mine. I stroked her fingers. It was quite dark now. On the hill tops for miles around one could see the Midsummer beacons burning.

I asked, 'Is it time yet?'

'You'll know,' she said.

The meat cooked quickly, and we ate it with our fingers, grease running down our chins.

'Who's that man with the princess?' I asked.

Branwen gave me a brief glance, then went on eating.

'Cormac the Charioteer. He's Dairmait's son. I'm afraid there'll be trouble. He wanted to marry Essylt once, but King Dairmait no longer needs Angus as an ally. He wants to form an alliance with the northern branch of his clan, the Uí Néill. The king will be furious when he finds out that his heir has missed the feast.'

The crowds had shifted and I could see the princess quite clearly now. She wore a white dress with a green cloak, and her hair, bound by a gold circlet on her brow, hung loose down her back. She sat very still, not eating or drinking, gazing at the man by her side, and listening to what he was saying with rapt concentration. He spoke fast, gesturing with his hands, and I thought that he must be telling her about something noble or exciting, a cattle raid perhaps, or some charge he had led. He was older than I, and very handsome, with a shock of black hair like a horse's mane, and a wide golden collar studded with jewels; so vigorous and full of life, that beside him Essylt seemed drained of colour, a reflection, an echo. Her eyes never left his face.

He finished the joint of meat he was gnawing, threw the bone into the fire, and wiped his fingers on his thighs. Then, taking her hand, he pulled Essylt to her feet.

Neither the king nor the queen was watching them. King Angus was on his knees, his eyes closed in prayer. Queen Deirdre lay back in the arms of some noble, who was kissing her lips. Cormac the Charioteer drew Essylt away from the fire, towards the gloom where the great fort cast its shadow over the hillside.

'Why are you watching them?' asked Branwen softly. She put her arm round my neck and kissed me on the mouth. I could hear music from the hall, shrill pipes, and the steady throb of a deep drum. She raised her head, 'Listen, the king's going to the goddess. Can you hear?'

I sat quite still, possessed by some deep nameless terror. I could see now that Angus was almost alone by the fire. Deirdre had disappeared, seeking, I suppose, like all the others, some dark corner in which to act out for her own delight the marriage of the king.

'What are you waiting for?' Branwen murmured. 'Is it possible that the wound has affected your manhood?'

'Don't mock me,' I said. 'Come into the dark with me, if you're not afraid, and I'll show you that I'm as good a man as any you've had.'

'Better, I hope,' she said, and I led her out of the fire-light.

I knew the direction that Cormac had taken with Essylt. If he's harmed her, I thought, I'll kill him; I killed Morholt, and he was older and stronger and more skilled than I. I'll strangle Cormac with my bare hands.

'Where are we going?' asked Branwen, tugging at my arm. 'Why not lie down here? How dark do you want it? Are you shy?'

'Shut up,' I said. 'I know where I'm going.'

We rounded the shoulder of the hill. There were no fires here, but the decorated bushes stood out boldly, luminous with gold thread. The music from the great hall had risen to a crescendo, with the bass drum echoing the beat of the blood in my chest. Branwen was saying something, I didn't catch what, when I heard the sound of a stifled scream. I shook off her hands and ran as I hadn't run for months towards the sound.

I almost fell over them, struggling together in a hollow. Cormac was naked.

I threw myself on to his back, got my forearm round his throat, and managed to force his head back quickly enough for her to slide out from under him.

'Run,' I told her, 'run quickly, back to the fires. Your father's there.'

I could feel her hesitate, but dared not turn to look at her. I felt the pull of my half-healed side and wondered if the wound had opened.

He said, through gritted teeth, '*Who are you?*'

'Drustan the Wanderer,' I said, before I thought.

'What is your interest in Essylt the Fair?' asked Cormac.

I could feel his bulging muscles beneath me. He smelled of sweat and leather, and the sweet oil he had used on his hair.

'I couldn't stand by and let you rape her.'

'*Rape?*' Cormac said, and began to laugh. 'You think the goddess has no power over Christian princesses?'

Suddenly he heaved himself over, taking me off my guard, and then he had me, sitting astride my waist, my arms pinioned against the earth by his powerful hands. Here in Erin they tied prisoners to three chariots, and drove each one in a different direction. Perhaps Cormac would keep my killing for his own sport. I could feel slow blood seeping through my tunic.

'*Damn you!*' Cormac said savagely, and spat in my face. I turned my head away and his spittle landed on my averted cheek. '*Damn you*, may you suffer all the bitterness you've just caused me to suffer. May it never leave you.' He said, '. . . damn you . . .' and spat again.

'Aren't you going to kill him?' Branwen asked.

I'd forgotten her. Cormac raised his head slowly. 'He'd be dead by now if it wasn't forbidden to kill tonight. I don't want to be an outlaw for the rest of my days.'

'Cormac the Charioteer, son of the High King of Tara, skulking in the forest and living on nuts, it's not to be thought of!' said Branwen with a laugh.

Essylt stood silently by, her face in shadow, watching us.

91

Cormac stood up abruptly and caught Branwen by the wrist. 'Are you for the taking?' he said.

She raised her mouth for a kiss, but bit him in the neck. He flung her down on the grass. As I staggered to my feet, I heard her snarling, and the sound of his curses beginning again; then suddenly she gave a shrill cry, stopped fighting, and began to moan.

I went to Essylt and took her arm. 'Come away,' I said. 'I'll bring you to your father.'

She pulled back and stood quite still, her eyes fixed on my face.

'Lady,' I said, 'be calm. You're safe now.'

'You!' she burst out. 'Always you! *Why* did you have to come here?'

I stared at her, unwilling to trust my eyes. She was so changed, so wild, so utterly unlike the timid Christian princess I had known, and so blazingly beautiful there in the darkness. *Was* it possible that she had gone with Cormac willingly knowing what he wanted?

She looked away, her lovely eyes veiled by thick dark lashes. Only her lips betrayed her by trembling.

'Essylt . . .' I said and reached for her hand.

She glared up at me as though I had wounded her. 'Take me to my father,' she said.

I dared not disobey.

King Angus was on his knees by the fire. Without another word to me Essylt joined him in his prayers. I sat down near them, bowing my head and trying to ease the pain in my side. Then suddenly we were roused by an ear-splitting din coming from the great hall, shouts and screams and wails mingled with curses. It sounded as if the end of the world had come.

I sat up. From the gates of the fort poured a great stream of nobles, some holding torches aloft, their clothes awry, some naked with flowing hair, all making that terrible noise. They flung themselves down on the hillside. A few knelt like Angus, shouting loudly heavenwards, but meeting with no response.

Behind came Dairmait, High King of Tara, recognisable

by his jewels, and with him was the priestess, covered only by her hair. Last of all hobbled a bent figure, thin as a skeleton, with the tonsured head of a monk. As he walked he rang his bell with steady reverberating clangour. Dawn was beginning to show in the east. The people all cowered before him, and he raised his bony arms to the sky.

'Cease your abominations!' he cried. 'The day of wrath is near. I, Ruadhan, have come to tell you so. Ignore me at your souls' peril; destruction will proceed from god. Every man's heart will wither away, tortures and pains will possess every one of you: god is fierce and full of indignation and fury. He will turn this earth into a desert and tear her sinners into little pieces.'

Such was the power of this monk that even King Dairmait cowered before him.

'You all saw just now,' he went on, in his ugly voice, cracked from much fasting, 'how the power of my god put out your heathen fires. I, Ruadhan, did it through his might. These fires shall never be lighted again. The stars will burn out; the sun will pour down from the sky in a hail of blood and flame; the moon will no longer shine. The Lord's coming is at hand. I fasted on Skellig Michael, and my Lord appeared to me in a cloud of light and told me to prepare for his second coming. So you must put out these pagan fires and cast out this whore of a priestess from among you. You must destroy the images of the old gods and worship only Christ who died on the cross for our sins. You must abstain from all fleshly pleasures; meat, wine, commerce with women. You must make yourselves ready for his coming . . .'

There was a great deal more of the same sort, and while he harangued them, the people never ceased to cry and wring their hands, grovelling on the earth in the fury of their self-abasement. The priestess ran away, but Dairmait stood rooted to the spot, pale with fear. At last Ruadhan turned to him, and pointed his fleshless, misshapen finger at the High King.

'And I curse you also, King of Tara, and all your kin, the pagan Uí Néill. You have done abominable things tonight, for which an eternity of pain cannot be punishment enough. The very stones of this proud fort will crumble and rot. The time will come when Tara is nothing but a grass-grown mound.' And he rang his bell three times to strengthen his curse.

So we went home silently in the first hours of dawn, chastened and afraid, like dogs after a whipping.

'If I had my way,' said the queen bitterly, 'that man would be stoned. I don't force myself into monasteries to show the hermits the error of their ways. Why should this stinking monk presume to instruct *me*? I don't give *that* for his blood-and-thunder god.'

'Oh mother,' said Essylt, who had been weeping silently all the way, 'don't speak like that. You'll be damned.'

'How does it come about, sweetheart, that your new dress is so torn and muddy, if you didn't feel the power of the goddess tonight?'

Essylt turned away and veiled her face.

# *Fourteen*

The fort opposite the oakwood,
Once it was Bruidge's, it was Cathal's,
It was Aed's, it was Ailill's,
It was Conaing's, it was Cuiline's,
And it was Maelduin's.

The fort remains after each in his turn,
But the kings sleep in the ground.

Essylt laid down her harp, and sat, her head bent, not looking at me.

'What is that song?' I said. 'I never taught you that.'

'I made it,' she said shyly. 'Is it right?'

I laughed. 'You'll be a master poet yet.'

We were sitting together, as we often sat, in her bower, with her ladies spinning and chattering in the room beyond. I gave her a piece of writing that I had done, but she could find no fault in it.

'What will happen now I can teach you no more?' I said gently. 'Perhaps it's time for me to go away.'

She raised her eyes to me slowly, and if I had struck her she could not have betrayed more pain or surprise. 'You're *going?*'

'I must. The year's ending. Soon it will be too late to set sail.'

'But where will you go? Oh . . . Will I ever see you again?'

Her face was like a pale flower with rain on it, and her forehead was innocent, untroubled. But I remembered the mud which had daubed her white dress when she lay on the ground under Cormac.

95

'Who knows?' I said. 'I've nothing to give you, lady.'

'I ask for nothing,' she said, very low. There was silence, and she added. 'When I'm at Taghmon I'll pray for you every day.'

It was my turn to be moved. 'But you mustn't go to that place! The rigours of the life would kill you inside a year. You'll marry some nobleman . . .'

'No,' she said. 'I never will. How can you understand? How can you know what it's like to have for your father a saint, a good Christian king, and to long to be like him . . .? And yet to have for a mother a woman who is given heart and soul to the old religion. There are two selves in me, and they never stop fighting!' She broke off. 'But I don't seek your pity. If you must go your way, then god speed you . . . But remember princess Essylt.'

Back in my room, I found that I was weeping. Her grief had woken mine, against my will. There was more danger here than in my broken sword, and, as Cerridwen had warned me, more wounds than one.

I lay down on my bed and thought of her, overcome by hopelessness, and a weary sense of fate.

And then, as I lay still, I realised that my bed felt strange. The hard shape of my sword, which lay between my pallet and the stone bench it covered, and which I could always dimly feel through the thin layer of straw, was subtly altered. I got up, stripped back the pallet, and looked. There lay the sword with its chipped blade; but instead of the hilt lying at the head end, where its contours were softened by my pillow as well as by the straw, the hilt lay towards the foot, and I had felt it under my knees.

Someone had been searching my room.

I thought, the time has come, I must go tonight. When they're all asleep I'll turn horse thief again and make for the coast. I'll take a passage on the first ship that casts off, whether she's bound for Powys, Kernow or even Armorica; it's all the same to me. I won't tempt fate any further.

I gathered my things together, and hung the largest cauldron to boil over the fire. To help heal the wound,

Queen Deirdre had made me bath in tepid water mixed with some lotion of her own. There was nothing I could do until night, and I might as well make use of the time to have a last bath. While the water boiled, I sat and practised my writing, and kept my thoughts resolutely away from the princess.

I tipped the steaming water into the tub, added enough rain water from the butt outside to cool it, and put in a good measure of the queen's green ointment. Then I stripped off my clothes and sank into the sweet-smelling water.

For a while I lay staring into the fire, then a sound behind me made me turn. Queen Deirdre stood in the doorway, with Branwen behind her.

'Ladies —' I began. The queen came into the room and I saw that she held a short sword in her right hand. Her lips were drawn back from her teeth in a snarl of rage.

I stepped out of the bath, snatching my cloak and wrapping it round my left arm as a shield. But my right hand was empty.

'Traitor!' hissed the queen. 'Vile murderer of my brother Morholt!'

I backed towards the fire. She jabbed at my breast with her sword. I heard Branwen laugh.

'Wait,' I said. 'How can you be sure that I'm the man?' I could feel the heat of the flames on my back.

'How not?' she cried. 'Who but I tended his body? Who but I washed him? Who but I pulled out from his cleft skull the splinter of metal from the sword that killed him? They told me his murderer was dead, but I kept the splinter, sensing one day I might meet the man whose sword was broken.'

'My sword is broken . . .' I said.

'. . . and the splinter fits.'

Branwen laughed again and Queen Deirdre came for me. She was quick, but not so quick that I couldn't reach behind me and pull the poker out of the fire. It was red hot, the handle seared my hand, but I thrust it towards her, and she jumped back, kicking the bath and slopping

97

water over the floor. We moved slowly, our feet slipping on the wet stones. I was sure it was Branwen who had found my sword, and I feared now that she would take it from under the pallet and attack me from behind. Without taking my eyes from the queen I managed to manœuvre so that she had her back to the door, and I could watch Branwen.

'Queen Deirdre,' I said, 'let me speak to you alone. You are a noble woman, and you come of a brave kin; don't kill me naked and unarmed. Let me at least explain my deed to you before I die. Grant me this one request. Your skill gave me life once —'

'Once was too much, traitor,' she said, but I could see that her first murderous rage had passed, and she was remembering that we had been friends.

'Branwen,' she said, 'go and fetch the king's bodyguard. Hurry.'

Branwen went sullenly.

'Was it she,' I asked, 'who found the sword?'

'She heard you tell Cormac your name. That was stupid.'

'I had other things to think of at the time,' I said.

She looked at me speculatively. The sword did not waver; the poker was cooling, but I could still give her a heavy blow if she came at me.

'Essylt told me that you saved her from rape. It was an interfering thing to do.'

I started. 'You wanted Cormac to have her?'

'Wanted? I'd half hoped he might. It was my dearest wish to see her betrothed to him, heir of the High King of Tara. What chance has she got here? But Cormac will never marry her now. I thought perhaps if she had a son by him . . .'

'She's only a child.'

'Better be Cormac's mistress than shut herself up at Taghmon and wear a hair-shirt for the rest of her days. If Morholt had lived I wouldn't have feared for her so; but *since you killed him* there's been no man at Dun Ailinne worth the name.'

As she said this she jabbed the sword at my breast. A

98

trickle of blood ran down. She raised the point to my throat. We heard the tramp of feet outside, and Branwen called, 'I have brought the guard, lady.'

'I'm a man worth the name,' I said urgently. 'If you let me live I swear I'll protect your daughter.'

Queen Deirdre's mouth flickered in a wry smile.

'It grieves me that I killed your brother,' I went on, 'for I respect and honour you. I had no choice but to fight him, the task was put upon me by King Mark my uncle, and it was fate that Morholt died. He was the stronger. I should have died. It was only by your skill that I lived. Can't you take that as a sign from the gods?'

'Gods?' she said, and spat. 'There are no gods,' and she was suddenly weary, an old woman. She lowered the sword. 'No,' she said. 'No. I won't kill you, Drustan. It is true that none of this was your choosing. I can't hate you.'

I knelt down, brushing the hair from my neck to give her a good aim. 'Strike now,' I said, 'or promise there will be peace between us.'

'Get up,' she said. 'Get dressed. You're already too vain of your fine body. Peace? None of us have any hope of peace . . .'

I kissed her hand and put on my clothes. 'May I bid the princess farewell?'

'No, you've caused her enough grief. She needs the protection of a warrior. I thought you might be such a man.'

'Do you think so still?'

'You are my brother Morholt's murderer. If I find you within these walls at sunrise I will have you put to death. Go now, Drustan. Torment me no more.'

'I will leave you his sword,' I said, 'to remember me by.'

# *Fifteen*

Once at the harbour I waited for a ship bound for Kernow, and after a peaceful voyage arrived at Castle Dor unheralded. I was unprepared for King Mark's joy. He said that they had all presumed me dead, having heard no news for a year.

That year seemed to have made all the difference between us. When I left we had been man and boy, now we were equals; even in some subtle way I seemed older than he. I told him everything that had happened to me in Laighin, leaving nothing out, not even the things which did me no credit. He asked me many questions, especially about Essylt.

Then he told me that my father and Cerridwen were both well, and their sons, and that she had borne him a daughter in the summer, who had been named Arianrhod.

At last I was almost asleep in my chair, so he blew out the lamps and lay down by the fire. So passed my first night at Castle Dor.

I woke before dawn, because I was not really comfortable in the chair, and looked down at the king sleeping at my feet and felt a sharp pang: he looked peaceful and happy, and I felt suddenly caged, like a wild dog which boys bring indoors and try to train as a pet. Yet King Mark was a good man, noble and clear-sighted, with a quick guileless mind; and if he wanted love from me, it wasn't the kind I had looked for from Myrddin, as if one of us had been a woman. But even so, Mark wanted too much.

I'll stay here the winter, I thought, then move on.

Mark and I fell quickly into the companionship we had

known before Morholt's coming, and I sent for Gorvenal to come from Kanoel to take me in hand, for I was sadly out of condition, and anxious to begin training again. Cynmor came too, and brought me a present of a new sword. He had heard tell how I had lost the other one. He too was moved to see me, but even with him I felt the same constraint. I thought, perhaps it's because I've been to the gates of death and back again. Other people matter less to me.

Mark broached the subject of marriage to me soon after. Cynmor had returned to Kanoel, and we were playing draughts together by the fire; his followers lounged about the room drinking and throwing dice, and Segward and Van had their heads together over their wine cups in the corner. They had been less than pleased at my return. Mark was never alone, could never be alone. He had been used to it, of course, from his childhood, but one could see it fretted him. He always withdrew as far as possible from his followers. Now he made sure they were out of earshot and then said abruptly, 'While you were away I fell into sin.'

He was watching my face. 'Did you, lord?' I said.

He pondered his move. ' Drustan, don't you feel any need to be baptised?'

'Why? You're the only Christian I've ever met whom I've admired. And Hywel too, I suppose,' I added, but I'd almost forgotten Hywel's existence.

He knew better than to badger me about it. 'You've no mistress, have you?'

'No,' I said.

' I admire your chastity.'

I shrugged. It was no use trying to explain to him that fear and disgust are not admirable. He moved his piece over the board, neatly dislodging several of mine. 'Last winter,' he said, 'I took a mistress. I used to go to her in secret. It was very difficult, I had to make excuses, hunting expeditions . . . It sickened me, but I burned for her. I couldn't think of anything else . . .'

102

He'd stopped concentrating on the game, and if he wasn't careful I was going to win. 'Why didn't you marry her?'

' She's already married.'

I looked at his face, the fine regular features, the fair curly beard, the level grey eyes, the broad forehead. It had not occurred to him to banish the husband and marry the wife. Yet King Maelgwn of Gwynedd had married the young wife of his own sister's son in just such a way.

'Who was she?' I asked.

'Segward's wife, Cunaide.'

I threw back my head and laughed aloud. 'Good for you,' I said.

It was a bitter winter, snow lay on the ground and the streams froze. I thought I'd die of idleness. I wrote and fought with Gorvenal as much as I could, but my strength had come back in full now, and I could feel the new power throbbing in my muscles, longing to be tried. I was very evil tempered.

Mark outlined to me his new schemes. Now that he was free of the due to Laighin he wanted to renew old trade.

'When the Romans were here, Kernow was rich,' he said happily. 'It's only since the barbarians came that merchants have been frightened away. We must lure them back, repair the roads . . . Do you think it might be possible to dig *underneath* the ground for tin? I've heard that it's mined in other places.'

'You'd better go out with your shovel and try,' I said, and felt empty pleasure when the smile left his face. 'I'm sorry,' I said, 'I don't know what's the matter with me.'

'It's dull for you here.'

'No duller than anywhere else.'

'Weren't you contented at Dun Ailinne? Surely the princess Essylt —'

'A child.'

'But beautiful?'

'Yes . . .' I said. 'She is beautiful.'

'Drustan, you know what Van and Segward are saying,

don't you? That I plan never to marry so that I can make you my heir.'

I laughed. 'But I'm certain to die before you, you'll live to three score and ten and be made a saint. Why don't you have them hanged?'

Mark sighed. 'They know a lot about politics,' he said.

So we fretted away the winter; Mark told me a little more about Segward's wife. Her husband had a farm not far from Castle Dor, but he seldom allowed her to come to court. When she did appear at supper in the hall sometimes I couldn't help staring at her, and found her eyes were often on me; but I had grown used to this. If one kills a famous warrior like the Morholt, and then returns from the dead, one is bound to become a hero. The ladies were always ready to make eyes at anyone new.

One day I found Segward's wife waiting for me on my way to practise with Gorvenal.

'Good day,' I said, and prepared to pass by.

She stood in the way and came out with a lot of stuff that I was sick of hearing, about how she admired my courage, and what a handsome face I had. I could never believe that, but I stayed and listened, and while I stood there, I thought, King Mark has lain with her, and she's beautiful.

I kept my distance, but I could smell her perfume and beneath that the strange female scents of her body. Her dark brown plaits were as thick as my wrists, and she had big dark eyes. As she leaned towards me, her breast moved under her dress, like an animal offering itself to be stroked. I was seized with desire so powerful that it was like anger. I frightened her. She pulled away, gasping, 'Not here!' She glanced round. 'Come to me tomorrow night. Segward will be with the king. Tomorrow, remember.'

'I'll come,' I said.

In that bout I beat Gorvenal to his knees.

Meanwhile there was the night to be got through. Each time I thought of her, I wanted her so much that I was sure I would betray myself. Not for the first time, I longed to strangle Segward with my bare hands.

When we were apart from the others I told Mark about the assignation. For a moment he sat quite still, then he said, 'You intend to go to her then?'

I nodded. 'I've always hated Segward, and I've never had a woman. Sometimes I think I never will.'

'Some of the saints,' said Mark, 'have lived and died virgins.'

'Women,' I said.

'And men too.'

'I've told you time and again, lord,' I said, 'I've no respect for your god.'

The others turned their heads and stared.

'For god's sake, Drustan,' Mark hissed, 'let's not quarrel *here*.'

'To hell with them all!' I cried blundering from my seat and upsetting the draughts board into his lap. It was an accident, but it seemed as if I had meant to do it. Mark went white. 'Get out,' he said.

'Haven't I done enough for you?' I said. 'I fought Morholt, didn't I, and nearly died of it, because all your parasites were too craven to risk their necks? Can you never stop ramming your religion down my throat?'

'You forget yourself, Drustan.' Mark's voice was calm and icy. 'Throw him out!'

During these months of comradeship I'd almost forgotten he was the king. Now he was nothing else. I had no other friend. Three strong lads seized me eagerly, and pushed me outside into the snow.

Roaring with laughter, they left me lying in the yard. There was no summons from Mark next day; I went and got drunk with Gorvenal. The hours passed very slowly, but I feared the coming of the dark.

When it was time to go, still warmed by the ale I had drunk with Gorvenal, I saddled Bane myself and set off over the frozen ground. The stars and moon shone brightly. I could have wished there was less light. But I felt wild and happy. I sang as I rode along.

I was still some distance from Segward's farm when suddenly two riders came out from under cover of the trees and drew rein in the roadway, barring my path. 'Stand and deliver!' they shouted. The hoods of their cloaks were up and they had scarves tied round their faces beneath the eyes, but even in the first surprise I noticed that they were well dressed for robbers.

'Get out of my way,' I said. 'I've no gold.'

'Never mind,' said one. 'We'll have that horse.'

'Dismount,' said the other, 'or you'll get what's coming to you.'

The first came near and tried to grab Bane's bridle, but I sensed rather than saw as I grappled with him, the other ride up behind with raised cudgel. I pulled hard on Bane's reins and he reared up, whinnying and striking out with his hoofs. They drew back a little and I could have spurred between them and probably got away, but my blood was up. I drew my sword.

Before they realized what was happening I rode at the first and ran him through the chest. He gave a cry and tumbled off his horse. He lay still in the roadway and the horse nuzzled at him.

'Pig!' yelled the other. 'You drew first! I'll swear that before god.'

'He shouldn't have got in my way,' I answered. Spilling with lust and anger like an overfilled cup I was ready for any infamy. 'Get ready.'

We spurred together, but he was quick, and my passion made me careless. He hit me on the shoulder. The weapon was wrenched out of his hand. I brought my sword down on his skull, the blow that had killed Morholt, but we were mounted and I hadn't the advantage of height this time. He gave a grunt and fell from his horse, but I knew I had only stunned him.

I sheathed my sword and rode on. My shoulder was bleeding freely and smarting in the cold air. No way to go to an assignation, but I would not turn back.

I was received with accustomed ease. The gatekeeper smiled as he let me in. The maid who opened the house door dropped a curtsy. 'The lady is expecting you,' she said.

I was unprepared for the children. She sat by the fire in

her bedroom with at least three clustered round her. There was a baby, about a year old, asleep in the cradle. When she saw me she kissed them all and the maid led them off to bed. As they left I could hear the youngest demanding tearfully, 'Why can't we sleep with Mummy tonight?'

Cunaide came towards me, her eyes shining, her hair unbraided and lying over her breasts.

'I thought you might not come,' she said, 'I'm glad you have. There's some supper ready. Let me take your cloak, then come to the fire and eat. You must be cold and hungry.' She undid the chain of my cloak and cried out when she saw the blood on my tunic. 'Oh gods! you're wounded. What happened?'

'Robbers. I beat them off. One's dead, I think. Let's not talk about it. I'm here, that's the main thing.'

We sat by the fire, eating meat and bread and fruit and drinking her husband's best wine, and the chill left me. I forget what we talked about, trivial things mostly. Her attitude to Segward amused me. She didn't seem to hate him at all, but thought of deceiving him as a game in which she pitted her wits against his.

'You see Segward doesn't care for me in that way.'

I raised my eyebrows. 'But you've got children.'

'Oh, yes, five. It's not difficult to get children. But he doesn't think of my pleasure, only of his own. Consequently —'

Our eyes met and we decided simultaneously that we had had enough to eat. But during our first embrace her words came back to me and I felt frightened. I held her away from me.

'You should know, this is the first time I've been with a woman.'

She began to smile, but tenderly, not mocking me as Branwen had done. 'And you so big and fine and such a hero,' she said. 'Then I won't suffer by comparisons, will I?'

So we went to bed. I opened her dress and her breasts overflowed my hands.

'Look, your shoulder!' she said.

The fresh wound was bleeding again; drops of blood spattered her fair-fleshed body, and stained the blankets under her. But I had gone beyond that and pain was part of my pleasure.

There was a knocking on the door post, but we didn't hear. The maid servant burst into the bedroom. 'Lady! Lady! Lord Segward is here with a bodyguard of men. Oh, lady, *please*, quickly or we're lost!'

I was dressed and kissed and bundled out the back way. I mounted Bane and rode quickly into the forest as far as I could. Then I threw myself off his back and lay on the ground looking up at the sky. I thought of Cormac the charioteer and his curse when I stopped him having Essylt at the *Feis Temrach*. I made peace with him in my heart. Now I could understand.

Gorvenal began dropping hints. 'One of the King Mark's men died the night you went courting.'

'So?'

'Run through the chest. His friend said they were attacked by a band of armed robbers.'

'That's common enough. Why the mystery?'

'What were they doing on the road from Castle Dor to Segward's farm in the middle of the night?' I said nothing. 'They were lying in wait for you! Can't you see, lord? The king sent them.'

I caught the neck of his tunic. 'Shut your mouth. Mark would never do a thing like that.'

He jerked angrily away. 'Why should I lie? The king was angry at the thought of you taking his old mistress. He wanted to stop you. It's as clear as day.'

'I don't believe it,' I said. 'Don't speak to me about it any more.'

Winter passed and spring came. King Mark's continuing displeasure pained me, and I was often lonely. I was on the point of leaving Castle Dor for Kanoel when the long-awaited summons came. Gorvenal was wary.

'What if he's sent for you to get his revenge after all this time? Some men are like that, you know, slow to anger, but once kindled their anger never burns itself out. Take care.'

'Mark isn't such a man,' I said, but how could I be sure? I'll know when he greets me, I thought, but I couldn't tell. Kings are so much among people that they develop a special face, like players. One cannot tell what they are really thinking. Mark greeted me kindly, embraced me and kissed my forehead.

'I've missed you, Drustan,' he said. 'Forgive me my anger. It was ignoble. I've fasted often on your account.'

I said, 'My exile has troubled me. But I'd hoped you might have changed your following.'

I jerked my thumb in the direction of Segward and Van, who hovered at the front of the throng, trying to overhear what we were saying. Mark's eyes narrowed. Was it my fancy, or were the lines on his face more deeply graven than when I had seen him last? His moustache was longer and made his mouth look sad.

'Don't antagonise them straight away,' he said.

I said, 'As I've proved, I'd give my life for you, but I won't lift a finger to further the interests of Van or Segward.'

Neither one of us referred to Cunaide, but I could see that he hadn't forgotten.

'It's my interests you'll be furthering . . . I sent for you to tell you some good news, Drustan. I've decided to marry.' I clasped the hand he held out to me. 'There was a time,' he said, 'when I hoped to live without a wife, as a Christian should. There was a time, too, when I hoped to make you my heir.' I started to protest, but he raised his hand and I fell silent. 'You're my sister's son, it would have been quite in order. But I came to see that it would not be wise. So I will take a wife and, with god's blessing, get children.'

'Who is to be your wife?'

'It isn't arranged yet. That's where I need your help. I want to marry Princess Essylt of Laighin.'

'*Essylt?*'

'Why are you so suprised? Political union with Laighin would benefit us immeasurably in the way of trade, as my advisers have long been pointing out. King Angus is in need of an ally. Essylt is a Christian princess, modest and fair, as you yourself have told me. What more suitable match is there?'

'And have you or your noble advisers' – I turned and bowed to them; they glared at me – 'by chance got any designs on ruling Laighin when Angus dies? You know she's his only child?'

'That isn't my intention,' Mark said. 'You should know me well enough to realise that.'

I stared at him. 'What do you want me to do?'

'Go to Dun Ailinne and pay court to Essylt for me.'

'What makes you think that I'm qualified to be a go-between?' I almost said *pimp*.

'You have visited Dun Ailinne before.'

'And was nearly murdered by the queen.'

'She gave you your life. Drustan, you're the only man I can ask.'

Surely he'd asked enough of me: I would be risking my life a second time for him. Was it possible that he was sending me back to Erin in the *hope* that I would be killed? And if this wasn't Mark's motive, surely it must have been in Segward's mind. My blood on his wife's blankets can't have given him much joy. He was quite capable of putting the king up to this.

'I've had a special ship built,' Mark was saying. 'The sails are painted with birds, and the oars are banded with gold. On deck I've had them make cabins, so that the princess and her ladies can travel in luxury. The ship's waiting in the harbour, full of gifts, ready to sail as soon as you give the word.'

'How could you be so sure that I wouldn't refuse?'

'I've always had the greatest admiration for your courage,' Mark said.

# *Sixteen*

So once again I took ship for Erin. Last time I made the crossing I was alone and near death; now I had companions, fine food, luxury. We rode into Dun Ailinne with great ado, and I demanded to see the king. I was haughty and refused to give my name. I sat on my horse and waited; I wanted King Angus to realise that I was doing him a favour; I had no intention of approaching him like a beggar.

We waited for some time. It was raining and the people stared at us uneasily. At length a man came out of the hall. He was alone and the crowd parted sullenly to let him through. I had expected King Angus but this was a young man, no older than myself. As he drew nearer I recognised him: Brendan, my opponent on Ynys Môn, the Morholt's younger brother.

'Dismount,' he said. 'Pay your respects, whoever you are. I am the king.'

I kneeled. 'I am Drustan the Wanderer,' I said.

'The man who killed my brother! I should have slain you on Môn, when we were boys together. I should not have let you live,' but he spoke wearily, and the energy that had made him so formidable a fighter was dimmed. Too much has been put on him too soon, I thought. It was the same for Mark. And I found it in my heart for the first time to be glad that I would never be a king.

'Stand up,' said Brendan. 'Why have you come back?'

'I've come in peace. Entertain me and my men according to the laws of hospitality, and we can talk.'

'We have scarcely enough for ourselves,' he said, 'but you shall be fed.'

While we were eating I asked how King Angus had died.

'In a raiding party led by Cormac mac Dairmait.'

'And the queen?'

'She is alive.'

'May I see her? My errand concerns her.'

I was shocked at the change in the queen; she looked haggard, old. Behind her sat Branwen, nursing a cat.

'Why have you come back?' muttered Deirdre. 'Isn't there trouble enough? Would Dun Ailinne be in peril if Morholt still lived?'

'Lady,' I said, 'when you spared my life I gave you a promise. I have come to honour the promise I gave.'

The queen looked up. Branwen smiled derisively; the cat was purring on her lap.

'What was this promise?' asked Brendan.

'I gave my word to protect the princess Essylt.'

Deidre rose to her feet. 'So you think *you* can save Laighin from devastation? You have come back to marry Esslyt.'

I clenched my fists. What a fool I had been not to have foreseen this!

'I have come to ask for Essylt in marriage,' I said, 'not for myself, but for my uncle, King Mark of Kernow.'

Branwen whispered, 'You were hoping for a miracle, lady. He runs away at the sight of a girl.'

'King Mark?' cried Deirdre angrily. 'And what has he to offer us?'

'He's a great king,' I said. 'He is rich and powerful, a good man and a Christian.'

'But would he send us troops? That's what we need, troops and money.'

'The ship I sailed in is loaded with gifts.'

Deirdre shook her head. 'I don't like it.'

Branwen said, 'But what is there for Essylt here? Cormac will never marry her; she's the princess of a ruined kingdom.'

'Ruined!' cried Brendan. 'I am the king, and while I live Laighin will never be a ruin.'

'You're not immortal,' Branwen said. 'The Uí Núill are. They breed like maggots.'

Queen Deirdre said to me, 'Remain at Dun Ailinne. Give us a few days to consult Essylt and discuss this.'

I asked, 'Where is the princess?'

'She's at Taghmon,' replied the queen.

The Uí Núill attacked twice while we were at Dun Ailinne, and I doubted if the fortress would hold out against them much longer. Consequently, I was anxious to get away. What negotiations were conducted among the royal family I don't know, but at length the queen informed me that Essylt would marry King Mark. I sent a messenger to Castle Dor with this news. My task remained to fetch the princess from Taghmon and escort her to her waiting bridegroom.

When Deirdre bade me goodbye, she said, 'You are a harsh man, Drustan, but I could find it in my heart to wish that you had come for Essylt yourself.'

'I'll never marry,' I said. 'Farewell.'

Branwen was to accompany the princess to Kernow, and on the journey to Taghmon I tried to ask her about Essylt's feelings in the matter.

'If you don't know,' she said, 'then I'm not going to tell you.'

'Sulk then,' I said. 'I shall be glad when this whole business is over.'

Essylt said, 'You've come back.'

We sat in a bare room in the religious house, and she wore the undyed garments of the nuns, but her beauty shone out like the light of a lamp.

'I've come to take you to Kernow,' I said.

She rose, and went across to the little window, standing with her back to me, staring out at the softly falling rain. She was small still, and slender, but I could not help noticing that the breasts which lifted her plain dress were full now. She said nothing.

I went on. '. . . This marriage will make you happy.'

She said with sudden passion. 'There is only one marriage that could bring me joy! This marriage to King Mark never will.'

'Believe me, lady,' I said. 'King Mark is a good man. He's a Christian. He's handsome and kind. Cormac would have used you harshly; King Mark never will.'

'Cormac . . . ?' she said distractedly.

For a moment her mouth trembled and I thought she was going to weep, then with bleak dignity she said, 'My mother and the king have been indifferent to my pleading. Like you, they think that in Kernow there will be everything to make me happy. They don't understand they are sending me to hell.' Then, with a sudden movement, she knelt at my feet, and the hood of her robe fell back, so that her bronze curls tumbled over her shoulders. 'Drustan,' she said softly, 'if I ever meant anything to you at all, don't refuse what I ask.'

'I'll give you anything I can,' I said.

'Then for god's sake,' she cried, 'leave me here and go home.'

'How can I?' I said. 'I've given my word to your mother the queen and to my uncle too. I can't betray them. And you? You don't really wish to stay here?'

'More than anything in the world,' she said. 'And if you had any feelings you would leave me alone.'

'But Essylt —' I reached out my hand to help her up, 'I want your happiness.'

She sprang to her feet. 'Don't dare touch me! Leave me! Oh, leave me . . .'

'Essylt, dear Essylt,' I said, 'you'll be happy, I promise you will. You'll have everything you could want.'

'Will I!' she said. 'No. Never.'

And then, with a flash of bright hair, she was gone.

Queen Deirdre was not a woman to be thwarted. Less than a week later I set sail for Castle Dor . . . with princess Essylt.

I did not understand how she could have changed her mind so utterly in such a short time. In place of the pale, drably-dressed novice who had pleaded so bitterly for me to leave her at Taghmon, was a laughing, lovely girl, with low cut dresses and painted eyelids.

On the evening of the third day out we were playing dice in her cabin, and I said to her gently, 'Are you glad now that you left Taghmon?'

For a moment her smile slipped and there was bitterness in her eyes. Then she said lightly, 'I could not fight them all. I prayed, god did not listen. Perhaps my mother is right after all, and it is the old gods who are all-powerful. Who knows?'

Something in her voice made me shiver. The lamp had burned low and threw strange shadows on her face, making her grey eyes seem very large and luminous. She had on a simple dress, sea-green in colour, which accentuated the whiteness of her skin; and across the bridge of her nose, as if they had been painted with pure gold, were countless tiny freckles.

She questioned me about Castle Dor, and I spoke on dreamily, almost hypnotised, as my eyes kept returning to the lamp flame, very low now, and to her great eyes, and to the deep, shadowy, mysterious cleft which her dress, partly unlaced, revealed between her pale breasts.

'It's growing late,' she said. 'Drustan, will you drink some wine with me before we say goodnight?'

I nodded. She took two golden cups from a chest, and set them on the table. Then she brought out a small flask of wine. 'My mother made this,' she said, pouring the clear honey-coloured liquid into the cups.

She gave one, very slowly, to me.

I raised my cup to her. 'A pledge,' I said, and my words filled me with sudden, unnamed horror. I stood quite dumb, fighting my fear, while Essylt watched me un-moving. But the terror disappeared as quickly as it came. The wine was strong and sweet. 'To your happiness,' I said and drank, as with a swift movement she also drained her cup.

She came near to give me more wine. My head was spin-ning. The ship was tossed about by a sudden swell, and as the waves rose and fell our hands touched, and I looked into her eyes, which were grey as the sea and fathoms deep.

I touched her mouth. We drank the last of the wine from the same cup. I touched her mouth. I kissed the parting of her hair, and felt her shudder, and drew her into my arms.

The ship was buffeted by the waves, and the cabin pitched from side to side. She clung to me, and I was drowned in the flood of my desire. I could feel her heart beating hard against mine. I tried to rouse her, tried to ask her what she wished, but her eyes were tightly shut and I had only her hands to talk to me and the silent message of her lips.

I barred the door, slipping the silver pin into the sockets that Mark had ordered to be carved so his gentle bride might have privacy on her wedding voyage. But I was a madman. This memory didn't move me one jot from my purpose. Her hands guided me to the bed and I unlaced her dress, and when I couldn't unfasten her petticoat she said, 'It doesn't matter,' and I tore it from neck to hem.

Then I was frightened, but her desire guided me. I touched her and it seemed that my hands knew things I did not.

She said, 'Yes . . .'

And I said, 'What about Mark?'

She said, 'It doesn't matter.'

It seemed that nothing existed outside ourselves. So I took her. It was as if our bodies had known each other many times before, we understood each other so well without speech. She was as reckless as I, and the end for both of us came together; then I lay in her arms, and woke slowly, as one wakes from a dream. But this wasn't a dream. Her sweat was warm on my chest.

'I love you,' she said.

'I love you,' I said; and it was true.

If my body had not joined with hers I might have lived my whole life in innocence of this love, but I had broken her virginity and mine, I had known her, I had penetrated without mercy into every part of her being, I had had her utterly, sparing neither myself nor her and the necessity of this love weighed me down like a curse.

'I'll always love you,' I said. 'There is no one else for me now.' It was true.

I turned on my elbow to look at her, marvelling at her beauty. Her face was calm as the drowned, except for the half smile that lingered at the corners of her mouth. I kissed her and felt the smile fade under the searching of my kiss.

Then the world came back to me and I was afraid.

'What are we going to do?' I said.

'Don't think of that yet. Oh, please, Drustan, let's be happy, now at least. You are glad, aren't you?'

'Of course,' I said, although I knew that I was no more than half glad. Love was so final a word, like fate and death. It made me afraid.

'You see, I knew you didn't care for me at all. It was like this with me from the first, I think, all the time we were together at Dun Ailinne. When Mother told me it was you who had killed Morholt, I tried to hate you. But I couldn't, I just prayed that you would come back. And then . . . oh Drustan . . . Why didn't you come for me yourself?' Her voice broke on the last words.

'Because I've been a fool,' I said. I could not bear to hurt her, she had loved and wanted me all the time I thought I would never find a girl I could love. Now I had, and it was too late, and she mustn't know. I could never tell her that my feelings were born of this hour, this bed, for then she would think it was only because she had given herself. It wasn't that, but it had taken the sweetness of her body to salve the wounds of my own.

'Hush,' I said. 'I love you. Let's make the most of what we have. Leave all the rest for later; there'll be enough time for it. Did I really please you? I've never lain with a girl before.'

'Is that true?'

'I swear it.'

She kissed me. 'You did please me, yes. So much that I was almost frightened.'

We lay and talked softly, but not for long. Then we loved again, and it was my turn to be frightened. Union with Essylt took me beyond my body, beyond hers, to ecstasy that was a vision and a trance. Afterwards she wept. '. . . Drustan, I'd like to die now.'

I tried to protest, but the words went unspoken. I knew she was right, as she had been right all along, and that there was no more to be said.

She was brushing her hair. She asked me, 'How old is Mark?'

'Five and thirty.'

'And is he . . . strong?'

'Strong as a horse, so far as I know. His father Cador died young though. So did his sister, my mother.'

'It's wicked to think like that!' said Essylt. She embraced me and we stopped thinking.

But at the back of both our minds, I'm sure, was a small hope that perhaps what we felt for each other was a will-o'-the-wisp thing that would not last. We'd given ourselves to each other as completely as we could. The completeness of it terrified us. Sometimes one or the other of us would draw back from the brink. My whole life! I thought. Not my whole life a slave. Just until she's married, then I'll go away. Or she, crying out in my arms, would be freed from me and think perhaps, Mark may be more handsome . . . and I'll be rich . . . and a queen! Afterwards we'd weep, begging silent pardon for our faithlessness, but the hope persisted, for we were as yet unused to wearing love's yoke. I have seen newly broken horses, apparently tamed and docile, taken with a sudden fit of bucking and rearing, as if they can't believe that one day they won't be allowed to go running in the fields again, free and alone.

'There's something I must tell you.'

'Don't speak.'

'I've gone beyond the point where I can keep silent. Drustan, Drustan, listen to me.'

'I'm listening.'

She got out of bed and put a cloak round her. It was dawn, and the sea was very calm. Grey light filtered into the cabin. Essylt picked up the empty flask from the table. 'This wine,' she said. 'My mother made it.'

I was sleepy and stretched lazily, tossing the hair from my neck. 'You told me.'

'She made it for me to drink on my wedding night. You see, I told her that it was you I loved, that I never could love Mark, so she brewed the wine. It was a love philtre.'

I sat up slowly, shaking my head to clear it. 'Essylt . . . What are you saying?'

She sat on the edge of the bed. She shivered and was afraid to look at me, but her voice went steadily on. 'She told me to drink the wine with Mark. She said it would bind us together, all our lives. That we could never love anyone else . . .'

I put my fingers under her chin, and tilted her face to mine. Her eyes were clouded now. Her mouth was a little swollen, and her skin was roughened by the stubble of my beard. Love had passed through her, like the wind through a field of corn, and her virginity was now a memory and a sheet stained with blood.

'Do you understand? I willed it. I did it knowing.'

'I understand,' I said. 'You've ended my loneliness. You've replaced it with something a thousand times worse.'

'You understand, don't you? I could never have married Mark?'

'Essylt,' I said, 'you must marry him.'

'Oh!' she cried. 'Oh! How cruel you are! If you'd struck me, if you'd wanted to kill me because of what I did . . . But to tell me that I must still marry him! I won't. It's impossible. You must take me away. How *can* I marry him now?'

I looked at her, and I loved and wanted her, but I knew beyond any doubt or question that she must marry Mark, and I also knew that, despite her protests, she knew it too.

'I've given my word,' I said. 'I am his sister's son. We have no choice.' And I began to weep.

She stroked my hair, pillowing my head on her breast.

I felt her tears on my neck, and because we were so newly lovers I was helplessly moved, and burrowed into her robe like an animal, into her gentle flesh, and forgot.

We had three days together. The cabin became our world and we tried not to look beyond it. But the day came when the breeze freshened and the ship made good headway, and soon we were sailing round Land's End and I tried to point out Kanoel to her. She pretended she could see, but we were too far out. Then we began passing the wooded estuaries of the south coast, and at last I recognised the port of Castle Dor, and the ship dropped anchor in the bay and we had our last night together.

She fell asleep for a little while and I thought of what she'd said. She had seduced me to this love and given me this pain; the pain of the last embrace, the last kiss, the parting. We should each of us speak to a thousand strangers and pass a thousand thousand hours of exile before we were together again. And we would have to suffer doubt and fear of betrayal. Would she still love me, wouldn't she hate me for deserting her? Would I find the same pleasure with another woman? Would I despise her for lying with me, and both of us for betraying the king, my uncle and her betrothed?

In the few moments while I stared at her sleeping face and longed for death, I hated her. She escaped, in sleep, the pain I felt. I saw the pulse throbbing in her slender throat, the transparent skin, the tiny blue veins in the eyelids whose lashes were darkened so that they showed long and black round the wide grey eyes, her tender mouth which I had bruised . . . I thought, destroy her and the pain goes too. I laced my hands round her throat. She stirred, the darkened eyelashes fluttered and she smiled at me.

Let her live, I thought, let her live and leave me. She doesn't belong to me. It's my own fault I suffer like a slave.

'Drustan,' she whispered, 'never leave me, promise. Kiss me. I fell asleep and dreamed you'd gone. I love you . . . Promise you'll never leave me.'

'Never,' I said. 'I promise.'

# *Seventeen*

She was married to King Mark, and though she was pale she bore herself bravely, and though I was nearly mad I never betrayed myself. Once I knew by her eyes that he had been to her bed, I wished with all my heart that I had forgotten my honour and taken her away when I could, for I knew then that a life of poverty as outcasts among peasants, even skulking in the forest and living off roots like outlaws, would have been better for us than this.

We were together a great deal. Mark said, 'You've told me, Drustan, when you first went to Laighin, how you taught Essylt to play the harp and she taught you to write. There's no reason why you shouldn't keep her company now.' And to Essylt, 'I never want you to feel lonely, or among strangers, my love. I can't be with you as much as I'd like. Let Drustan give you music lessons. After all we owe our happiness to him.'

But there was worse than this for us to endure. Mark said to me, 'Drustan, I've decided to have you proclaimed my heir.'

We were all three sitting by the fire and Essylt had been pouring wine for us. Her hand trembled suddenly and the wine slopped on to the table. For a moment I could summon up no logical excuse, then I remembered the old rumour-mongering of Segward and Van, still Mark's advisors and regrettably unmellowed by time.

'Is that wise?' I said. 'You remember, before, all the talk —'

'Before?' Mark reached across the table and took Essylt's hand in his. 'Before perhaps, but there'll be no rumours now that I'm married.'

121

'You'll soon have sons of your own, lord,' I said, trying to keep my voice steady. 'What's the point of naming me?'

'I'd like to think that if I died childless, or left a son too young to fend for himself, you'd reign until he was ready.'

'But I don't —'

'Please, Drustan, let me do this. You've done so much for me.'

He pressed his lips to Essylt's hand, and her eyes met mine wildly across his bent head.

An edict was prepared, duly written in Latin:

## DRUSTANS, CUNOMORI FILIUS, HINC PRONUNTIATUS EST HERES

That winter I divided my time between the king and the queen. I spent days with Essylt in her rooms, surrounded by her ladies as in the past, and I spent days sitting in the Council, or hunting in the forest with Mark. I slept in his hall, except for the nights he went to the queen, and then I didn't sleep. Sometimes I went riding in the darkness, sometimes I knocked up Gorvenal and made him wrestle until dawn, sometimes I turned away and cried. My bed was against the far wall of the chamber, near the door. It was easy to slip out unobserved, easy to stifle my noise against the cold stone wall.

On these nights I always thought I would leave Castle Dor, but when I saw Essylt the next day, looking so fresh and fair, I abandoned my plans for departure. But it was hard to keep the secret. I wanted her so, and the time on the ship seemed so far away. Whenever she came into the room my heart began to race. If she crossed behind my chair to fetch something, shivers ran across my shoulders and down my back; and when she was playing and I bent forward to hear so that her hair almost touched my cheek, it was as though our bodies remembered the delight they had once exchanged and strove to give their gifts again, even across the space that separated us.

One day we sat together in her rooms, Branwen and the

others a little way off. A small fire flickered in the hearth, but spring had come. I could hear the birds singing outside. Mark had gone to her last night and all there had been for me was the narrow bed and the cold hard stone which I clawed with my fingers.

She was sewing and I was reading to her from a Latin book. My voice had sunk into a monotone while my thoughts ran riot. Suddenly, I felt I could stand this half-life no more. I longed to shout aloud to her, but I dared not. I slipped into my reading the question, '*Regina, me amasne?*' 'Queen, do you love me?'

'*Ita,*' Essylt murmured softly.

'*Cur me crucifiges?*'

Shocked by my blasphemy, she gave a start and raised her head. I had accused her of crucifying me, but I read in her eyes all the answer I needed.

'Essylt,' I whispered, 'don't torture me any more. Either bid me leave here or bid me come to your bed.'

'Hush!' she hardly breathed the word.

We glanced at the ladies; heads together, backs to us, they were happily gossiping, oblivious of what passed between us.

'Essylt, I see his empty bed, I know he's with you . . .'

'*Don't speak of it!*' she hissed. Her face was pale, the golden freckles stood out over the bridge of her nose. She was cowed, terrified. Where was the reckless creature who had urged me to tear her petticoat, to take her flower: 'It doesn't matter.'

'Tell me you don't want me and I'll bother you no more.'

'I want you,' she said dully. 'I thought I could love you with my soul alone, but my flesh torments me.'

There was a stir among her ladies then and I went on with my reading. After a while I dared to stretch out my hand and lay it on her knee. A shudder ran through her as though I had burnt her. She had suffered too.

'Let me come to you.'

'How?'

'Let Branwen come for me. When *he* isn't there. She'll keep the door for us.'

'I'm afraid.'
'You weren't afraid once.'
'Things change.'
'I want you. Send for me. Promise.'
'Yes.'

So I went to her, but that first night was too short to satsfy us after our winter fast, and I went back again and again, and the more dangerous it was the more we longed to be together. We had a narrow escape when Branwen, coming to summon me, encountered Mark on the threshold; and another when, leaving her rooms dizzy with lack of sleep I fell down a flight of steps and had the guards searching until morning for the dawn prowler.

It was inevitable that sooner or later we'd be found out. I hoped that when it happened Mark would strike the blow himself and so be revenged on me for the thousand wrongs I'd done him. But Mark seemed cheerful and content, loving Essylt, his chaste wife, and me, his loyal nephew, and never dreaming of the evil we did him.

When the first rumours began to spread, like a vile plague, my immediate action was to question Branwen, for she had our lives in her hands. Mightn't it be to her advantage to betray us? Segward or Van would pay well for such information.

'Well, you bitch,' I said, 'who's been telling tales?'

She stared at me narrow-eyed. 'Not I,' she said. 'Do you think I want to see my lady burnt?'

'Maybe not your lady,' I said, 'but you don't care for me, do you? I spurned your offer at Tara, didn't I?'

'Cormac the Charioteer satisfied me well enough,' she said with a laugh. 'I've no quarrel with you, Drustan. You drank the queen's wine. This isn't your fault. But others sleep in the king's hall. Might not one of his bodyguard have noticed your empty bed?'

'I'll say I was with you.'

She shrugged. 'Much good you'd be to me with half your mind on her! No, I'll leave you to your undying passion, lord, and pray I never catch the same sickness. But if you take my advice you'll keep to your own bed until the talk has died down.'

So I kept to my bed, and let my blood rage.

But however modestly Essylt behaved, gossip hung over her like a cloud of smoke, and I noticed that other men were drawn to her by it. Denied her body at night I also had to shun her company by day. I felt like a great maddened bear, baited from all sides and unable to lunge at its tormentors. Sometimes my bondage seemed too cruel and I determined to break it, but I could not, could not . . .

There was at court a young man named Andret. Mark was his uncle, but on his father's side. Andret was slim and fair, and I could see that Essylt liked him. He made her laugh. They seemed to spend a good deal of time together. She ignored me and I suffered, thinking, can it be that she's a whore by nature? Perhaps she's tired of me and already taken Andret to her bed.

I told Branwen that whatever the risk I must go to Essyle that night. She told me that I was mad, but came to fetch me a little after midnight.

Essylt, being queen, had rooms as public as the king's, but from the first she had slept in a small private chamber, which adjoined the main hall. This room had a window which had been my almost nightly means of entry and egress.

'Stay here,' I whispered to Branwen, and she nodded sullenly. I often woke her as I jumped down just before dawn, but I couldn't blame her for falling asleep over her thankless task.

I braced my hands on the sill and pulled myself up through the window. The room was in complete darkness and there was no sound. I usually shed my boots and tunic and found my way naked to her bed, but tonight I did not.

'Light the lamp, Essylt, I said. 'I must talk to you.'

She obeyed and was revealed to me by the flickering flame of the lamp turned very low, sitting up in bed, a fur coverlet held to her breast, her hair loose over her shoulders.

Her eyes held mine in fear and longing. 'Drustan?'

I wanted her, and this augmented my anger. 'Essylt,' I said, 'where is Andret?'

'Andret?' she asked, all innocence and bewilderment. 'How should I know? Asleep, I suppose.'

'And how long will it be before Branwen leads him to your bed instead of me?'

'Drustan,' she said, 'are you sick? What's the matter? Why are you talking like this?'

'I've seen the way you smile into his eyes, the way you move your body towards him . . .'

It was difficult to quarrel in a whisper. My voice was rising. She laid her fingers across my lips. I felt the warm pressure of her breasts. I couldn't help pulling her towards me. 'You're a whore,' I muttered, stifling my anger against her flesh. 'You're a whore!'

She spoke very coldly and quietly. 'If I *am* a whore it's you who've made me one. I've never been with any man but you . . . and the king.'

'Do you swear that?'

'On anything you like.'

'On the cross, on my dagger hilt, on the heads of your unborn children?'

'Oh god, on anything you like,' she sobbed. 'Drustan, when will you believe me? I love only you.'

I gathered her to me, quenching her sobs against my chest. When she had quieted I asked more gently, 'Why do you spend so much time with Andret?'

She sat up, arranging her hair. She filled our cups and sat looking at me for a moment. Her face was set, she wouldn't cry again. 'You are right in a way,' she said. 'Andret loves me. Or he says he does. He hoped that the gossip was right and I'd give in to him easily, but I've managed to convince him that, although I like him, I'm a Christian lady of sincere virtue.' Her mouth twisted with these words, as though she was tasting something sour.

'Why not tell him to go to the devil?'

'Don't you see, I can't afford to make any enemies? You know as well as I do how dangerous our position is.' She lowered her voice, I could hardly hear it. 'If we're dis-

126

covered we'll both die. I don't want to die, Drustan, but I can't live without seeing you. I tried. I hate deceiving Mark, he —'

I interrupted, 'This is the truth?'

'Yes.'

'I can check on it with Branwen you know.'

'Listen,' she said, 'while you're accusing me about Andret, don't mention that girl's name to me. I have to live with her, listen to her, sleep with her. Sometimes I can hardly bear it, I want to scratch her eyes out. She's forever talking about you: "*Drustan*'s taller than any man here . . . *Drustan*'s as strong as an ox . . . *Drustan* killed Morholt when he was no more than a child . . . *Drustan*'s the sweetest singer in the world . . ." It makes me sick to hear her. Oh love, if it torments you to see me with Andret, it tortures me to see you with her. Why do you do it? Aren't I enough for you?'

'Wait,' I said, 'I'm not Branwen's lover.'

I took her in my arms. Morning was coming, and we'd worn ourselves out in quarrelling. It seemed that there had always been more sorrow than joy between us. I did my best in the little time that was left to redress the balance, and in the stillness after love told her I was hers only, and knew her mine, and resolved not to be foolish any more.

But my jealousy, like my desire, was constantly re-kindled. Soon after this I saw that Andret was holding her hand while they listened to some song of mine after supper, and afterwards I made her swear that she'd tell him to leave her alone, whatever the consequences. She told me that when she did as she was bid Andret had glared at her and said, 'Is it love of Christ or love of another that stands in my way, lady?'

'I blushed and said, "Love of Christ," and he said, "Is it Christ who visits your bed every night the king isn't with you?" Drustan, I'm frightened. He *knows*. We must be careful.'

But I was in so deep now that I could never keep away from her for very long.

# *Eighteen*

In summer there were always many hunting expeditions
in the Moresk forest. The game we killed was preserved in
salt to feed us through the winter when we couldn't hunt.
Mark went out often, though I had never thought him
especially fond of hunting, and I usually accompanied him.
If we went too deep into the forest to get back to Castle Dor
before night the whole party camped out. We took bows
and arrows to hunt deer, but when wild pigs were our
quarries we took the dogs, hunting nets and boar spears,
which were exceptionally long and heavy to withstand the
weight of the massive boars. During one of these expeditions I was rash enough to get myself stuck in the thigh. I
was too stubborn to let go my spear when the pig swerved
towards me, hoping that I'd have enough strength to drive
the point home single-handed. But I hadn't. The beast
trampled me down and mauled my thigh.

I was carried back to Castle Dor on a stretcher and saw
Essylt's face grow pale before I could wink at her to reassure her. But it meant I couldn't climb in at her window
for a while.

The rumours had subsided, but even so I could count
no man as a friend. Only Gorvenal stood by me, and even
he was taciturn and bad-tempered. I knew that Andret
would kill me if he had half a chance: if Mark had turned
against me they would have torn me to pieces. But he never
did. He spoke to me politely, even kindly, asking for a
favourite song that I had played him in the old days. But
he avoided touching me now; he never embraced me gently
as he had before, and the light of friendship had gone from
his eyes.

Another hunt was planned but I couldn't go; my wound

wasn't sufficiently healed. I lay flat on my back on my bed and hoped that they wouldn't be away the whole night. It was high summer, twilight lingered. Finally as it grew dark I sought out Branwen. I found her gossiping in the kitchen and drew her aside to the accompaniment of knowing looks from the maids and whistles from the young men.

'Tell her I'll come to her,' I said.

Branwen gasped. 'You mustn't! You can't, not tonight. The king suspects, he's given special orders.'

'What are they?'

'When the queen goes to bed Segward and Van are to sprinkle flour over the floor, round the bed, everywhere. It was Van's idea. They're out to discredit the queen, both of them, and they want you dead because you're the heir.'

'How do you know so much?'

'I keep myself informed.'

I had my arm round her waist, and I seized her wrist and bent it up between her shoulder blades. She gasped with pain.

'Tell me,' I said.

'I'm Van's mistress. Sometimes he talks.'

'It'll pay you to tell me what he says in future,' I said. I let her go. 'Tell the queen I'll come to her.'

'But what about the flour?'

'I'll jump,' I said. 'It's no great distance from the window to the bed.'

I made the leap easily, but that and the effort of climbing through the window opened the wound in my thigh. I didn't notice. Essylt had never seemed more beautiful or the night shorter. She's my soul, I thought, if I lose her, I lose my soul; if I'm cruel and base in my other actions an hour with her redeems me.

I left her the way I had come, with a headlong leap through the window. As I picked myself up and stood panting in the cool dawn air, I felt the blood running down my thigh in a hot heavy stream. I started back to the window to call to Essylt, but it would be too dangerous. 'The bed must be soaked,' I told Branwen. We had had no need of blankets, but I had pulled the fur over us once. 'Make sure the fur isn't stained —' I began, but she'd gone.

I limped back to bed and woke Gorvenal who bound up my thigh again.

'You're a fool, lord,' he said, 'do you *want* to die? Anyone could've told you that cut was nowhere near to holding yet. What possesses you, lord? For god's sake, let's go back to Kanoel now, before it's too late.'

At that moment we heard the guards blow their trumpets. The king was back early from the hunt.

I lay in bed and tried to sleep. I was bone-weary and my wound was hurting. Towards noon a boy came and said the king wanted to see me. I was feverish. I told him that as I couldn't walk the king would have to come to me.

A while later Mark himself arrived. He was freshly bathed and seemed rested. My face was swarthy with beard stubble and I could smell my own sweat, mixed with a woman's smell on me. I hardly dared look at him. He'd brought some food. After the slaves served it he told them to leave us and stay outside to see that we weren't disturbed.

He propped me up on a pillow and gave me a leg of chicken. 'Your man said you haven't eaten, have this. Is that leg worse? I thought it was almost healed.'

'So did I,' I said. 'I was bored to death not being able to come with you, so I went for a ride by myself and it opened up. Stupid of me.'

'Yes,' he said.

We ate in silence and drank the wine. Mark said abruptly, 'Drustan, do you remember, once I told you something I'd never told anyone else, about Cunaide, Segward's wife?'

'Yes,' I said. I thought, is he tormenting me on purpose?

'I've never got over my shame about her. Even now I still think of it. And she's dead, poor creature . . .'

'*Cunaide?*'

'Yes. She was only three and thirty.'

'I didn't know.'

'Sometimes I wonder if she's suffering for the things we did together . . . if even now —'

'Don't think of it!'

'But I must, for my soul's sake. Drustan, lately I've done something perhaps even more ignoble . . . Someone . . . *someone* has been telling me horrible stories, about you and the queen: that you have been going to her secretly, at night. He told me you have been lying with her in her bed. Copulating with her. Oh god, Drustan, I've half-believed him — so I made a plot with Van and Segward. They were to scatter flour round the queen's bed so that if any man came there I would see his footprints in the flour. And I camped not far away last night and came back early this morning to find —'

'What did you find, lord?'

'A whole host of footprints in the flour! The queen's bed stripped of all its covers. She told me she had screamed and woken up from a terrible nightmare. The poor child, it was my foul suspicions that gave her nightmares . . . But, Drustan, when I see her in her thin dress, so beautiful, I *want* her so . . . and oh god, I still suspect her of adultery.'

He put his head in his hands and began to cry. I stroked his hair. 'Lord,' I said, 'you're only human, try as you may. No one can be perfect, not even a king.'

'Wait,' he said and raised his face. 'I've something more to tell you. I did you another wrong, a long time ago. That too was because of jealousy. You told me you were going to visit Cunaide and I hated you because *I* longed to go and knew I must not. So I sent two boys to stop you. As god is my witness, I told them not to harm you.'

'I remember,' I said. 'I killed one of them.'

'Yes, but his blood's on me. It was all my fault. Drustan, forgive me.'

'I bled all over her sheets,' I said.

He started, and stared at me, not knowing if it was Cunaide or Essylt that I meant. And even I, feverish and guilty, could not be sure.

He said, 'Yes,' and then, stronger, '*yes.*'

We sat without moving. 'I'll go away,' I said, 'as soon as I'm strong enough.'

'You're strong enough,' he said. 'Go today.'

The spell broke and I was afraid. Why hadn't I kept my mouth shut? I could have forgiven him and he'd have been none the wiser, after all. 'Are you banishing me?' I asked.

He shook his head. 'But I charge you on your honour: don't come back until you'll do me no more wrong.'

And I thought: that is banishment.

He went then, and I left for Kanoel a few hours later in the back of a cart driven by a triumphant Gorvenal.

I thought of Essylt throughout the journey, so hopelessly that I began to weep. She's my soul, I thought, where can I go without my soul? *Drustan the Wanderer*: if a wound hurt as much as this, it would pain me to death.

# Nineteen

So began in earnest the years of my exile; my travels up and down the country from fortress to fortress, from court to court, in the hope that somewhere I might find a place to lay my head where sleep would come to me easily, where I would not dream of her. I even began to *want* to forget her, and thrust all my memories from me instead of cherishing them because they were all I had left of her. But whether I tried to remember or to forget, at last all thoughts of her coalesced into one: so that awake or asleep, at table, playing, singing, riding to hunt, or drunk, or even with another girl, Essylt was with me.

I remained at Kanoel only until my thigh wound had healed; my father never even tried to tempt me to stay. Older now, his thick hair was growing white. He knew that I was lost to him, and his thoughts had turned to Cerridwen's children.

As soon as I could I headed eastwards again. I left Gorvenal and went alone, riding Bane fast over the crumbling roads, trying to outstrip my thoughts. I avoided Castle Dor and turned north, travelling up the Hafren valley. The dark woods encroached farther and farther on to the track, and in the autumn stillness Bane's hoofbeats echoed between the trees.

The Romans had built these roads; the Romans were brave and strong and masters of much learning. But they had gone away, and many had perished under the attacks of the barbarians. Their roads were cracking. We remained, trying to piece together their learning and our own while the storm threatened. How long would it be before the Saxons tried again, pushing farther and farther west until they had conquered all the land? Arthur was dead; once I had dreamed of being such another leader, but I would never be a conquerer. My battle field was a bed, and my enemy a princess from Erin. I had nothing left for other foes.

I let my beard grow on the journey, to hide my jawline and my mouth, in case anyone should recognise the thief of King Maelgwn of Gwynedd's horse. Of course Bane and I would now have to part; but he would have an easier life back home in Degannwy with the grooms to feed him than he had had with me. In the night rides I had taken from Castle Dor to escape the thought of Mark and Essylt, I had broken his wind, but he seemed to bear me no grudge.

I turned him loose outside the gate and went into the fortress with my pack on my back like a pedlar. My name, I said, was Kai, son of Nimdor; for I'd become accustomed to this alias in Erin, as accustomed as a man ever gets to answering to a name not his own.

'Yes,' said the lord I spoke to, 'we'll hear what you can do tonight. We're in need of some new entertainments here; you're the first bard who's dared come since the plague.'

'You've had plague here?'

He nodded.

'How many died?'

'Too many: the queen and her little son, almost a third part of all the nobles.'

'And Myrddin the bard?'

The man laughed. 'Take more than a plague to kill that one off!' Then he crossed himself, as if afraid of his mirth.

King Maelgwn had aged greatly, and his eyes were hooded, as if he hardly slept. Now there was fear in his face, where before was arrogance and the custom of command.

The meal was half over when Myrddin arrived. He slipped in between the tables, bowed to the king and took his seat. I wasn't close enough to see him clearly, but he looked as if he hadn't changed at all. I wondered if he would remember me.

When the meal was over Maelgwn of Gwynedd summoned me to play.

'Something new,' he said, his voice hoarse and strangled, 'something new . . .'

I bowed. 'Of course, lord.'

I began to play. When I was with Essylt she had made me cut my finger nails because I hurt her if they were long, but away from her I had let them grow again, as all bards do, to gain pure tone from the strings they pluck. I lingered over the introduction as long as I dared. While I lay in bed at Kanoel I had made a song, not on any of the old patterns that I had learned, but my own song. I wondered if I dared tell it, for it would surely give too much away. Then at last I thought, I made it for her. I'll tell it, no matter if the king has me killed.

I said, 'There is a song, lord, that I know you have never heard before. It's the "Song of Drustan the Wanderer and his love for Essylt the Fair". Would it please you to hear it?'

The king frowned as if memory had plucked at his sleeve, but he nodded in a preoccupied way. I didn't look at Myrddin. I began but scarcely got through more than one verse. Tears were falling down my cheeks . . . I bowed my head and let my fingers slip across the strings in a harsh dissonance. I thought, I can't finish it, I have no more strength . . .

I felt an arm placed lightly round my shoulders.

'You must pardon the bard, lord,' Myrddin said, his well-remembered voice clear as ever. 'He's travelled over-much. I myself will undertake to look after him. I give you my word you'll hear the rest of his song tomorrow evening.'

There was a rustling in the hall, feet scraping along the floor, the soldiers rearranging their bodies as men do who have sat still for some time and are preparing for some more active amusement. But they were disappointed. Maelgwn of Gwynedd got up.

'Stand up, bard!' he said.

I wiped my tears away with the back of my wrist and stood up. I wished I didn't tower over everyone.

'I'm not the fool you took me for, I know that you are

Drustan, son of Cynmor, now calling yourself the Wanderer, for all your tales about Kai son of Nimdor. I know that you repaid my generosity to you by stealing my favourite horse. But no matter. If you had come back a year ago, I promise you, you'd be dead by now, or else praying to die. You can thank your stars that you find me a changed man. I have known sorrows of my own, and it's made me soft and indulgent towards others. May you find rest at Degannwy, Drustan, and forget your lady . . . Though god knows *I* never shall.'

With that he strode out of the hall.

'Drustan —' Myrddin said, 'I never expected to see you again.'

I found I was trembling. 'Let's go outside,' I said.

They made way for us. Out of the hall I felt better, I was able to smile at him. He took me to his house. Preoccupation with myself made me insensitive to him. 'Where's your wife and daughter? Where's Gwion?'

'All dead.'

'The plague?'

He nodded and began to cough. I saw that there were creases round his eyes, not the old marks of laughter; and new lines embittered his mouth.

'Myrddin —' I began, and stopped. There was nothing to be said.

'I missed it all,' he said, 'I was away in the north. When I got back they were dead and burned.'

I moved my mouth, words eluded me. 'Thanks for trying to help me just now.'

'I recognised you at once. Not by your playing, which has improved out of all recognition; no, by the way you held your shoulders. Did you know? A trick you have of hunching yourself up, trying to seem less tall. You must stop it if you intend to continue appearing incognito. It will give you away. Now, will you have some wine?' He had still the same light, rapid way of talking, but now the boredom was more real than simulated and the graceful movements weary rather than languid.

All earth's brightness is dimmed, I thought. Even

Essylt's eyes do not shine as they did when I first kissed her.

Myrddin came back with a jug and two wine cups. He filled them and raised his to me. 'To our old friendship, Drustan.' He drained his cup. 'I gather that you haven't been idle since I saw you last. How long ago was that? Five years, six?'

I thought of how I'd looked for him to come to the island, and how I'd grieved when he never sent me a message, not even a token that he thought of me. But why had I attached so much importance to it? Try as I would now, I couldn't remember. I had nothing to tax him with; whatever had been for me was over. It was too late.

After more wine and talk about our adventures since we saw each other last, he rose and came round to my side of the table. He stared at me a moment, then settled himself at my feet, leaning his head back against my knee.

I stroked his hair, which was freshly washed and shining, smelling of herbs. He tipped his head back and looked up at me.

'So Essylt the Fair is your mistress?' I nodded. 'And she's married to King Mark your uncle?'

'Yes,' I said, 'I can never go back, it would be death for us both.' I added after a moment, 'And him.' For it came home to me then that Mark loved me, perhaps as much as he loved Essylt.

Myrddin was watching me, his grey eyes clouded. I thought, it would make him happy if we could touch, but I can't. We are too alike; that somehow precludes touch. If it were Gwion, then perhaps, but Gwion's dead of plague. His ashes are laid in some chamber tomb. I should have said yes to him if I had had the chance. But now I am a woman's man. Essylt's man. I can't act out passion with Myrddin.

As if he had followed my thoughts Myrddin smiled, and delicately, so I hardly felt it as rejection, he shifted his weight from me and leaned on his elbow. 'You must tell me,' he said, 'more about the songs you've made.'

'Something I learned from Essylt made all the difference.'

He raised his eyebrows. 'And what was that?'

'She taught me to write.'

# Twenty

I went to live with Myrddin. He was not well; he'd caught the plague himself, and though he had recovered, it left him weak and with a harsh relentless cough that worsened as the winter dragged on. I tried to make him rest, but he was impatient with my solicitude. Of course I taught him to write, and in return he showed me new skills on the harp. We played together often, and once, when a particularly lovely combination of sounds vibrated in the air and then died, Myrddin said, 'If only there was some way of writing music, as there is of writing words. I suppose no wise man from Erin has found a means of doing that?'

I shook my head. 'There's your life's work, Myrddin.'

'Not for me,' he said, coughing. 'I'm too fond of pleasure to devote myself to such a task.'

I too had become fond of pleasure. Degannwy overflowed with good wine and the plague had made those girls who escaped conscious of the short time their youth and prettiness would last. Neither Myrddin nor I took a regular mistress, but we never went short of a girl; sometimes by choice we'd have only one and take her into bed between us, using her to exchange the desire that was never communicated by our own flesh.

My life with Myrddin was like a drug, the kind they brewed me when I lay near death from Morholt's wound, a drug compounded to make me sleep and forget my pain and the death that was coming to me. Sometimes, though drowsy with wine or poetry, or girls, I couldn't sleep. I lay in the dark, more and more awake, but not myself. An empty void. An ache. Only barely alive. Without my soul.

Spring came and with spring, as the snows thawed and the mountain passes were open again, Gorvenal arrived.

Essylt had sent Branwen to Kanoel with a message for me, and when Branwen knew that she'd missed me she tried to make Gorvenal start for Degannwy there and then. 'And by all the gods,' Gorvenal said, 'she knows how to coax a man! You may hanker after the lady, lord, but I'd recommend the maid any day.'

He had withstood her blandishments, however. It was too late in the year to make the journey; he had a wife and children to think of. This reminded him to ask after Blodwyn the cook. She had died of the plague. Gorvenal shivered. 'Unlucky place this. King Maelgwn, the Island Dragon as he's called, looks half off his head to me. Poor Blodwyn, she was a good woman, poor little lad too.' He blew his nose on his cloak.

'What was the message?' I asked.

'What?'

'The queen's message, the reason for your journey. You haven't told me yet.'

'Well, well!' he said, 'No more I have. The long and short of it is that you're going to be a father, lord. Probably already are by now. Congratulations.'

He thumped me hard on the shoulder and set to work on a vast plate of steaming food that Myrddin set before him.

I sat down. 'How could she be sure it's my child?' I asked. 'And why didn't she tell me herself before I left?'

Gorvenal masticated his mouthful thoroughly before saying, 'Branwen explained all that to me very carefully. Seems that it was the final arrow that felled the doe. A Parthian shot you could say!' He laughed uproariously.

I gritted my teeth. 'How can the queen be sure it isn't Mark's child?'

'Because King Mark is given to fasting, lord, like all good Christians.'

I sat silent while he finished eating and began to pick his teeth with a chicken bone. Myrddin came back with a jar of his best wine.

'Let's drink to the baby,' Gorvenal said. 'Here's hoping it lives. And to the queen too.'

140

'If *she* lives,' I said bitterly.

'Don't fret about that, Drustan,' Myrddin put in.

I turned on him. 'She's as slender as a child.'

'She could bear your weight, couldn't she, lord?' said Gorvenal. 'She'll bear your child all right. It's always the big women that suffer most, the ones with big hips that look as if they could drop a calf without much trouble.'

'I hope to god you're right,' I said.

I had meant to give her nothing but joy.

Gorvenal told me that Branwen herself had promised to come to Degannwy as soon as the child was safely delivered and the queen was strong enough to be left. Gorvenal decided to stay with us. 'Branwen will find us sooner or later.'

'You think she'll keep her word?'

'I do.'

I shrugged. 'We'll see.'

Summer drew on but Branwen did not come. I thought: Essylt's dead and no one dares tell me.

The Midsummer Festival came and went. Maelgwn of Gwynedd gave a great feast. The holiday lasted three days with jugglers, tumblers and bear baiting. Myrddin and I both came near to losing our voices, even though we soothed our throats with honey cordial. I was drunk most of the time. When I had sobered afterwards I began to make plans. I decided to stay at Degannwy until the end of the season. If the king was demanding of his poets at least he was generous with his gifts to us. Then, before the autumn weather closed in, I'd persuade Myrddin to leave for Erin.

On a stormy day late in the season, when I was wondering if I hadn't left it too late and would be stuck at Degannwy for the winter, Branwen arrived. I knew immediately that it was she, though she was wrapped in a dark blue cloak and the hood obscured her face.

I ran forward and snatched the reins from the slave who held her horse. 'Branwen!' I said, 'for god's sake, what news?'

'Drustan, I'm so pleased to see you . . . They're both safe, never fear.'

She slid off the horse's back and we embraced, tears running down both our cheeks. 'Come, quickly,' I said, 'tell me everything.'

Branwen moaned. 'Give me a chance! I'm as saddle-sore as a new cavalry man, and my hands are blistered all over. I must have a drink and a square meal, Drustan, or I won't have the strength to tell you a thing.'

I took her to Myrddin's house. The lady and the two slaves who had accompanied her got themselves a meal in the kitchen. Branwen settled herself against the cushions on the couch and Gorvenal kissed her heartily. Myrddin fetched us all some wine and stood listening politely.

'Well?' I said, half-mad with impatience after she had greeted everyone, exclaimed at the luxury of the house and drunk a full cup of wine.

'Put the poor man out of his misery, for Mithras' sake, girl, and me too. Is it a son or a daughter? Quickly now!'

'A little son,' said Branwen. 'He's well and strong.'

'What about the queen? Was it an easy birth?'

A shadow crossed her face. 'To tell the honest truth, lord, no, it was not. Two days and nights the poor queen suffered. For my part I thought she was tired to death, and that she'd go with the baby still inside her. I've seen that happen often enough.'

I clenched my hands. After a moment I found that the long nails had cut into the palm. I wiped the blood on my tunic. 'Go on.'

'Towards evening on the second day the pains seemed to ease. I'd been with her since it began, you understand. I was tired to death but she was frightened to be left alone. The king was praying outside.'

I thought of Essylt lying on the bed where we had lain so often together and of Mark's vigil in the hall beyond; her groans clearly audible through the hangings.

Branwen said, 'We talked about you. She couldn't raise her voice much above a whisper then, poor lady, and the other women had gone away, so it was quite safe. I tried to

142

encourage her. I told her how proud you'd be to have a child, and how much you loved her.' She wiped her eyes. 'I thought she was dying. I wanted her to go quietly without all the palaver of monks and confession. So I just sat and held her hand, and she said, "What colour are his eyes do you think, Branwen? Blue . . . or green . . . or grey?" She closed her own eyes then and I thought it was over. Then suddenly she gripped my hands like a vice and said, "It's coming, Branwen, quickly! It's coming!" And the next moment without any help from me, there he was, your son. And no wonder he cost her dear. I never saw such a great strong baby, and she as narrow as a boy.'

Gorvenal blew his nose. I said, 'Stop snivelling. What's there to cry for? Fill my cup, Myrddin.'

Branwen accepted more wine. 'I would've come before, lord, but the queen had childbed fever and I had to nurse her.'

'She's recovered, you're sure?'

'I wouldn't have left her otherwise.'

'When was he born?'

'The week before Easter.'

'The sign of the Ram,' said Myrddin quietly. 'He'll be a soldier, Drustan.'

After this we had a meal and drank, and Gorvenal took Branwen to bed. When they came back we all laughed and drank some more and the next thing I knew she had slipped off with Myrddin. Gorvenal was saddened by this, and as just then I was full of happiness, I tried to divert him by asking him about his old adventures, though I'd got them all by heart long before when Hywel and I used to listen to his tales by the hour. In the course of the conversation it came out that he wanted to marry Branwen.

'Why?' I asked astonished. 'She's half your age and as light as a cork. Besides, what about Breisa?'

'You underestimate Branwen,' he said. 'She's got twice as much sense as most women, and she'd go through fire for you and the queen.'

It was inevitable that sooner or later my turn with Branwen would come. Gorvenal fell into a drunken sleep.

Myrddin was plucking a tune on his harp, totally absorbed, he might have been alone in his house. Branwen touched my hand and whispered, 'Come.'

I owed her this. She's been loyal to me without reason, and without thanks. So I took her into my bed. I closed my eyes against the coarse black hair, the wide high cheek-bones, the slanting black eyes, and took her as I took all women, to invoke *the* woman, as priests invoke their gods.

She was not ill-pleased, but sighed and stretched like a cat when we had done.

'Talk to me about her,' I said.

She laughed aloud. 'What a pair you two are!'

'I'm sorry,' I said, wondering belatedly if I'd offended her. 'Branwen, tell me, are you going back to Essylt now?'

'If I can get back before the roads are blocked.'

'Don't tell her, will you, about this? It might grieve her.'

'It would grieve her, Drustan. She's very jealous about you. No, I would never say anything to hurt her.'

'Branwen, you'll stay with her, won't you?'

'Yes, I'll stay with her, and protect her as long as I can.'

I said, 'Thank you, Branwen,' and kissed her lips.

When Branwen left Degannwy, Gorvenal went with her. I did not dare risk writing Essylt a letter, which might be stolen or intercepted and incriminate both of them, but I sent her a gold ring in the form of two clasped hands. I sent nothing for the child. I had nothing to give him, not even a name: that would be for Mark to choose. What would it be? Cador, after his father? Paul, after the hermit who baptised him?

I longed to see my son. When I pictured him at Essylt's breast I could feel no remorse, or compassion for Mark, only my own triumphant joy. I hungered for him, and when I thought of the lonely miles, the mountains, the rivers, that separated me from my own flesh, my heart ached.

'I must go,' I told Myrddin. 'I must go to Castle Dor,' but winter had trapped me at Degannwy.

'How *can* you go back?' Myrddin said.

The snow fell steadily, wrapping us in its cold, white winding-sheet.

One night Myrddin's coughing seemed worse than usual. I heard him clearly from the next room where I lay, unable to sleep. At last I got up, wrapped my cloak round me, and lit the lamp. I went through to his bedroom. He lay propped up on pillows. His hand was at his mouth and I saw that his fingers were stained with blood.

I set the lamp down by his bed.

'Myrddin . . . Why didn't you tell me?'

'This is the first time, tonight. But I've been expecting it. I've had pains in my chest all winter.'

We looked at each other, and he began to cough again. The blood flecked his hair. I fetched some rags.

'Drustan,' he said, 'I'm afraid.'

I envied him his fear. I took him in my arms. 'When spring comes you'll be better, you see!'

I said no more about leaving.

If I could have given him my strength I would. I nursed him as best I could, but there was not much to be done. The winter dragged on.

One day it seemed as if spring might really be coming. Myrddin was in good spirits, and appeared stronger than he had been for some time.

'Take me out with you,' he said, as I put on my boots. 'I've been shut up indoors for months.'

I thought the fresh air might do him some good.

'Lean on me,' I said. 'We'll go slowly.'

I took him by the easy track, but before we'd gone very far I knew I'd made a mistake. His breathing was harsh and loud, his face white.

'Want to turn back?'

He shook his head. 'I want to see the sea. I can hear it all the time —'

He coughed. 'Lean on me,' I said. I half carried him over the frozen earth. We reached the cliffs.

'Here,' Myrddin said, '. . . it's so cold . . .'

145

I could see the island, far out, reflecting the light from its smooth pale face.

'Look!' I said, pointing.

He was leaning heavily on my shoulder. 'Drustan . . .' he said.

'Look,' I said. 'There's Môn out there!'

He turned his eyes from my face and scanned the sea, took a half step forward and stumbled. He would have fallen if I hadn't caught him in my arms. He had fainted; his head was turned, his face obscured by the fall of long fair hair. I turned his face to mine, a trickle of blood ran from the corner of his mouth.

'*Myrddin!*' I said.

He died. I heard the last breath rasp from his mouth, and looked if I could see his soul as it flew away into the air. The air was frozen and still, but I could see nothing.

I picked him up in my arms and walked back slowly over the ice.

# Twenty-One

Spring had come, but Myrddin's death chilled me to the bone. Might not my son also be dead, a handful of pale ashes in some chamber tomb? And Essylt? Was her body still warm with life, pliant as water, my harbour, my home?

I thought, her body is and always has been my home. I must go home.

'Drustan!' said Mark, 'is it really you? Why didn't you send us word? My dear Drustan!'

Essylt sat with her hands folded in her lap, a matron now, her bright hair covered, demure and serious. But I had seen the brief blaze of her eyes answering mine, in a glance of recognition so fierce that I knew she had forgotten as little as I.

Mark had aged; I saw it in his slower movements, the thickening of his neck. But his joy at seeing me appeared unfeigned.

'Where's the prince? Drustan, did you know; I've a son!'

Like an arrow to the heart, I saw him. How can Mark not realise? I thought, he's so dark. I saw a sturdy child, big for two, with a shock of black hair and his mother's pointed face, her freckles. They'd given him a little wooden sword with a gilded handle, which hung from a belt around his waist, and he already wore a golden band round his forehead. Mark's heir. He'd waited for him long enough.

'What's his name?' I asked.

'Constantine,' Mark said, and I was angry that he had been called after a Christian king.

'This is your cousin Drustan, son,' Mark said.

147

Essylt said, 'Kiss him, Conn.'

I picked up my son in my arms, holding him hard, close to me. He stared at me, unwilling to be overawed, then his solemn face broke into a slow smile and he reached out and grasped my beard. I kissed him. I could feel the strength already in his small limbs. If he grew as tall as me they'd be hard put to it to explain that away. 'Go to your mother,' I said.

He went and stood by her chair and she hugged him. I saw the line of her hip under her dress as she turned. How soon can it be? I thought.

I stayed at Castle Dor for two days and spent nearly all this time with the king.

Mark questioned me closely about my wanderings. 'How I wish,' he said, 'that I'd seen the wonders that you've seen; the cursing of Tara, Maelgwn of Gwynedd's fortress . . . ! But tell me, are the men of Alba still heathen?' I nodded. 'Think of it,' he cried, 'what a task to undertake; bringing the word of god to the savage north, baptising the fierce Picts. If I were free to choose, Drustan, that's what I'd do.'

It was suddenly clear to me that Mark should have been an evangelising monk, not a king. In the dangers of such a mission he would have found happiness, he could have purged himself of the sense of sin and guilt that chafed like a hair-shirt beneath his nobility.

I asked him about politics. Modred still ruled at Camlon, but didn't seem likely to continue much longer. Mark had begun a series of defensive ditches round Castle Dor in case the Saxons overran Lloegrys. People called the first rampart the Giant's Hedge.

Mark asked if I had come any nearer to god and I thought of Myrddin's death. 'Every step I take seems to lead me farther away,' I said.

He looked at me sharply, and for a moment I was frightened that he could read what was in my heart. 'I pray for you, Drustan,' he said. 'I feel I've failed in my duty towards you. You're my sister's son and yet you wander the land like an outlaw.'

148

'It suits me,' I said.

'Drustan,' he said gently, 'when you went away last time we parted in anger. There is no anger in me now. Won't you stay here, make your home with us? There's no man in the world so dear to me as you are.'

I could hardly speak. 'I can't stay,' I said. 'It's impossible . . . but, thank you, Mark. Thank you for your generosity.'

'It's nothing,' he said. 'At any rate, please take this bracelet as a parting present. Wear it for me, I insist . . .'

Near tears, I left him.

But I wanted her, and I wanted my son.

Gorvenal and Branwen had married and they lived now on a small farm, near to Castle Dor. I went there.

'I've come to ask your help.'

Branwen, heavily pregnant, put a hand on her belly, and Gorvenal drew her to him. I thought, with an obscure, shameful pleasure: they're afraid of me.

'We did not think to see you again,' Branwen said.

'Myrddin died,' I said, 'not I. I've come back to see the queen.'

Gorvenal sighed. 'And what part do you expect us to play in this, lord?'

'Branwen's her friend, isn't she? What is more natural than that the queen should come and stay with you, especially as Branwen's with child.'

Gorvenal turned away. Branwen gave me a bitter look. 'I had hoped to be free of you,' she said.

'Go to Castle Dor tomorrow,' I said, 'and tell Essylt that I'm waiting for her here.'

I lay on my bed, idly plucking at the strings of my harp. It was a warm evening and I could smell supper cooking, mingling with the sweet-sour farmyard odours, and the scent of the honeysuckle which hung in rich clusters round my narrow window.

Essylt had promised to come tonight.

The playing could not soothe me, my fingers were stiff and clumsy. I lay face downward on my bed and tried not to think, not to listen, not to be. At last I heard a light tap on the door. I jumped as though I had been burned. It was Branwen with a jug of wine.

'There is a carriage coming up the track,' she said. 'The queen will come to you as soon as Conn's in bed. Do you want some supper?'

'No,' I said. 'Yes . . . all right.' I couldn't remember having eaten at all that day. I might feel calmer with something in my stomach.

Branwen went away. Gods! I thought, remembering the women I had had since the queen, and how each one had seemed stupid, or too sharp, indifferent or over-greedy, compared to her. And each time I lay empty and alone with some alien body in my arms, I'd thought of her. Suppose memory had played tricks on me, suppose she had changed?

The door opened and Essylt came in. She moved hesitantly.

'Drustan?' she said, and I heard the catch in her voice, the rough edge of fear.

'It's all right,' I said, 'I'm here. Wait, I'll light the lamps.'

I took up a taper, and carefully, one by one, touched it to the wicks of the lamps in the three-tiered holder. Then I blew out the taper and turned to her.

'Why not sit down?' I asked, indicating the low bench. 'Branwen brought us wine. Will you have some?'

Her voice failed, she cleared her throat. 'A little,' she said.

'Was your journey comfortable?'

'Yes, the roads are dry. Conn slept nearly all the way.'

I gave her wine. 'Please take off your veil, I prefer you to be comfortable.'

She had already slipped the light travelling cloak from her shoulders, and I noticed her dress. In the past she wore green, because of her hair, but this gown was bright rose pink, embroidered with gold at neck and hem. She took off her veil.

I drank and then looked at her over the cup. She blushed. I saw the colour rise in her cheeks and dye her neck and bosom. This time she won't come to me, I thought; this time I must woo her. And though I had had much experience with women since I saw her last, her beauty awed me and I found it hard to speak. I wondered what changes she was finding in me, what new scars.

'Thank you for telling me about the child,' I said.

'I thought it was right that you should know. Besides —' she broke off.

I waited for her to finish but she would not. 'You've no more children?'

She shook her head. 'I don't think Mark will give me a child.'

I longed to ask her about other lovers, but dared not. Branwen came in with the food.

'Is Conn still asleep?' Essylt asked.

'Fast asleep, don't worry. I'm going to lie down beside him myself, so he won't fret for you.'

Essylt did no more than pick at her food. I wasn't hungry either, but I spooned some of it down. Branwen had cooked chicken stew with celery and herbs and it was good. We ate ripe pears afterwards and washed our fingers in the water Branwen had left. Essylt hardly touched her wine.

'Let me play to you,' I said.

When it was half-done I saw that she was crying. I put the harp away and knelt in front of her. I took her hands away from her face and held them in mine. 'What's the matter?' I said.

'Oh Drustan,' she said, 'why did you come back?'

'If you want me to go away tell me so,' I said.

'No, I don't want you to go. I . . . I hoped that you might come again. I've been lonely. I thought you must be dead.'

'Death sent me back to you.'

'. . . and I thought that you must have travelled so far away, and seen so many fine fortresses, and met so many beautiful women.'

'Essylt,' I said, 'all is nothing that I've had.'

'And I,' she said.

The nights we stole so often at Castle Dor had always seemed short, but this night time had no meaning. We kept the lamps burning and talked louder than whispers;

151

and when I took her she cried out aloud as though her joy was itself holy and nothing to be hidden. If I had had doubts and mistrust, I lost them then. Like pure metal in a forge we melted into each other, the break was mended, we were whole.

'Oh Drustan' she said, 'I'd forgotten. I thought of you so often, tried to remember. But memories are nothing either, are they?'

'Isn't it like this with Mark?' I could ask her anything now.

'No,' she said, 'he does it as though he hates me. He loves me, I know; he's very kind to me. Even when you went away before, he didn't punish me, although, of course he suspected. He punished *himself* for his suspicions. And he punishes himself for his passion. It makes me feel unclean.'

'I'm glad,' I said, 'I'm glad. *I'm glad* I'm the only one who knows what you're really like, like this.'

She laughed. 'I don't know myself like this. Kiss me again. It's strange, you free me from my body. You make me go beyond myself . . . almost, as if I know what it will be like when I'm dead, when I am part of god . . .'

I lay and gazed at her, seeing how bearing the child had changed her body, threading her belly with delicate tracery whiter than her skin, slackening the taut round breasts, darkening the tender nipples.

We talked about Conn.

'Branwen told me that you almost died.'

'Oh that, that was nothing. I won't be such a weakling next time.'

The enchantment that held us was so strong that we even laughed about having another child, and I insisted that she must bear me a girl with hair as bright as her own.

'I know how the earth feels,' Essylt said. 'In a dry summer when there's been no rain the ground is parched. When the rain does fall the earth can't drink enough, isn't satisfied until the land's running with water.'

'Do you believe that the end of the world is coming?'

'The monks are always telling us so. While you were

away another monk came, Samson. He built a church near here. I gave my best dress.'

'Why?'

'A penance, they said I should. It was very expensive, you see, it had jewels sewn into the borders.'

'Essylt, if the world does end, I'll come to you, wherever I am. If you ever need me, you'll send for me, won't you? And if I ever send for you you'll promise to come?'

'Don't talk about going away. Not yet. I'm staying a week.'

'Won't Mark . . . ?'

'He knows that Branwen's pregnant. She needs me. He understands.'

'You don't believe you'll suffer for your sins, in hell I mean?'

For a moment her face twisted. 'Mark does, and so did Angus, my father. Angharad was always telling me that the wages of sin is death, and Samson often took that text for his sermons. But Branwen says it's a lot of nonsense, and Deirdre my mother used to laugh at the idea. I sometimes think that Branwen and Deirdre are right, and yet the Old Religion frightens me. I love the stories about Christ, his healing and gentleness. Sometimes when I'm praying I feel such comfort and stillness, as if god is listening to me and that he will look after Conn, and you too, Drustan.'

'Does he answer your prayers?'

'You've come back, haven't you?'

'Drustan, I've been thinking' – (She had greater stamina in love than I. She always vanquished me.) – 'if we told Mark everything, don't you think he might let us go?'

'He'd kill us.'

'No, I don't think so. It would grieve him terribly, but he wouldn't hurt us, I'm sure.'

'He might not hurt you, but he'd have me tortured, I've done him too many wrongs. You don't understand men.'

'I think he'd forgive us. We could go away.'

'Even if Mark let us go,' I said, 'what about Conn? He's made Conn his heir, hasn't he?'

Her face darkened. 'Yes,' she whispered, 'he loves Conn.'

'What if we told him Conn's my child?'

'He loves Conn,' she repeated. 'He wouldn't let him go.'

'Would you come with me and leave Conn behind?'

'Don't ask me,' she said, 'I can't even think about it!'

When dawn came we slept lightly, still conscious of each other. We hadn't been asleep long when Branwen came to wake us.

'Lady,' she said, 'Conn's awake, he's asking for you.'

Essylt yawned and raised herself up on her elbow. 'Yes... of course. I'll come. I can sleep later.'

My first impulse was to keep her with me. 'Please,' she whispered. I took my arms away and she climbed sleepily out of bed. Branwen wrapped her in the robe she'd brought.

'Come back soon.' For a moment I was filled with jealousy of the child, the new rival, this fresh obstacle between us.

'As soon as I can,' she said. She sounded weary and I felt ashamed. After all, I could sleep now. She must attend to her child.

'Try to get some rest.'

'I'll see to that,' Branwen said, 'as soon as she's quieted the boy. I'll look after him then.'

She opened the door. We could hear angry sobs from across the hall. Essylt went to Conn without another word to us.

The parting drew near and seemed unreal.

'Can't you stay?' I said. 'Send word. Say Branwen is sick.'

'How can I? I daren't, Drustan, he'll guess.'

'I won't let you go,' I muttered.

'I'll come back soon. When her baby's born I'll be able to stay longer. Please.'

'I won't let you go,' I said. 'You belong to me, not to him.'

'You're hurting me!'

At times the only way we had been able to express our passion was by pain, but this was different, there was no play in it. I wanted to kill her.

'Stay with me!'

'No, I won't!'

Aghast, we recoiled from the brink of hatred.

'I'm sorry,' I said. 'I know you must go.'

She left amid drizzling rain, and it was only then that I realized how fine the weather had been during their stay.

'Well,' said Gorvenal, seeing my stony face, 'was it worth it then, all the trouble?'

# Twenty-Two

The harvest was over. Blackberries hung, heavy and ripe along the hedges. I found it hard to live through the hot, empty days, and I hated all those about me.

Branwen gave birth to her baby one night at the end of the summer, cheerfully and with little fuss, and I had only a few hours to wait before Essylt arrived. She was full of concern for her friend, but I could see from the look she gave me that our parting had been as bad for her as it had been for me. She hadn't brought Conn, and I was sad not to see him; part of my longing remained unassuaged by Essylt's presence, and I realised then that I had missed him too without knowing it.

'I thought it was best,' she said, when she'd kissed Branwen and admired her fine son and we were at last alone together. 'He is talking so much more now that I just couldn't take the risk a second time.'

'Where is he?'

'With Mark and his nurse. I've never left him before . . .'

She stood staring at me with clenched fists, and in the moments before tears washed her face she looked as though she hated me.

'Oh love,' I said, 'please don't cry.'

'I've cried so much for you,' she said; but she let herself be comforted and gradually, making love together, we forgot our child.

She stayed for nearly a month, and we were happy. I can say no more. Of course she pined for Conn and I couldn't risk going for even a short ride, but despite all this we were happy.

'If we had all our lives together,' she said, 'do you think we'd still feel like this?'

'No,' I said, 'there'd be times when we'd wish we were never married. You'd have a child a year and get fat. I'd be battle-scarred and even uglier than I am now, and we'd be poor.'

'Even so,' she said, 'I wish it could be like that. Do you?'

'Yes,' I said. 'Must you go away?'

'He has Conn,' she said.

'When will you come again?'

'I don't know . . . Oh, don't ask me. I daren't come too soon, it would arouse so much suspicion. Van is dead, but Segward hates me as much as ever, and Andret —'

'*Andret?* Is he still at court?'

'Yes, and he is still dangerous.'

I looked at her as she lay beside me, her hair spread out over the pillow, and could almost make myself believe that if I closed my eyes she would be gone when I opened them, for I knew that all too soon I would be lying there alone, and the pillow would hold no trace of her.

On our last night together Essylt gave me a ring. 'I've been keeping this to give you in return for the one you gave me.' I slipped it on to my third finger and she said, 'If this is all we're ever going to have will you still be glad?'

'Glad?' I laughed, 'What a question! Kiss me.'

But she raised her head from the kiss. 'Don't you ever intend to . . . marry?'

'Marry? No, never. Does that satisfy you?'

'Yes.'

I watched her go: what premonition had made her ask me that? Partings grew worse, not better. How could I stand a life of it? I should move on, I knew, but I couldn't tear myself away. I was as surly as a caged bear. Branwen and Gorvenal were out of patience with me and left me alone.

She had recovered quickly from her baby's birth. The boy was called Finn, after Erin's famous hero, Finn mac Cumhail, and seemed strong and healthy enough to warrant a hero's name.

I began to pester Branwen for news, begging her to go

to Castle Dor and thinking up a hundred pretexts for Essylt to come to the farm; but Branwen refused to listen to me.

'You're a grown man now, not a boy. You only torment her. Make up your mind to leave her alone.'

'How can I?'

'Choose a good girl and marry her. Forget the queen.'

'You seem to think that others are as faithless as yourself!'

'I've been a true wife to Gorvenal, even if I was wild before I married him.'

'Wild! You lay with every man between here and Dun Ailinne.'

'Do you really think,' she asked, 'that this love of yours, this madness, is *good*? It's destroying you, Drustan. Do you want it to destroy all those about you?'

'I don't give a damn,' I said.

But sometimes I was frightened; it *was* like madness. Would she never come? Winter passed. One day I saw that the snowdrops had started to open. I would wait for the daffodils to come, and if I had heard nothing from Essylt by then, I made up my mind to go to the Castle, whatever the risk, and speak to her for myself. But as if she knew my mind a message came just as the first buds were opening; it was for Branwen, asking her to go at once.

I waited sleepless for her return.

'Is she coming?'

'Yes, she's been sick. She's coming to rest here.'

'How soon?'

'A few days.'

'What sickness?'

'She miscarried a child.'

It seemed like punishment, I would have loved to see her big-bellied and beautiful, pregnant by me. I asked, 'Is Conn coming?'

Branwen nodded. 'She wouldn't leave him again.' Gods above, I thought, let our luck last!

One could see she had been sick. Her skin was very pale and there were dark rings under her eyes. Conn had grown. He was wide awake when they arrived, and ran into my arms. I never thought he'd remember me, but she had seen to that, making me the hero of a long series of bedtime tales.

So once again she was in the room that had seemed like a tomb without her. I feared to touch her, she'd become so frail.

'I don't sleep well,' she said. 'Drustan, I couldn't keep away. When the daffodils started to bloom I couldn't bear our being apart any more. . . I'm so sorry about the baby.'

'Please, don't cry,' I said. 'It doesn't matter, nothing matters except that you're here.'

Even in my arms she was frightened. 'I shouldn't have come. They suspect. I think Andret guesses. You see, he still wants me. He's jealous of you, he wants to kill you!'

'Hush!' I said. 'It doesn't matter. Nothing matters when we're together. Remember what you promised, about the end of the world. Pray for it to happen now, while we're together.' She shivered and laughed. 'Take off your dress,' I begged, 'and all that heavy jewellery. I won't do anything you don't want, but let me feel you naked close to me. Here, let me, I'll do it.'

So she stood passive like a child, while I unclasped the gold collar studded with turquoise from round her slender neck, and slipped the great turquoise and gold earrings from the narrow lobes of her ears. Then I unlaced her yellow dress and pulled it off over her shoulders, and undid the fine linen petticoat, and unbound her hair.

She stood naked with her hair curling over her shoulders and down her back.

'You're beautiful,' I said. 'Please lie down.'

She slipped into the bed, and I stripped off my clothes and got in beside her. She curled up against me, cold as ice. '. . . You're so warm!' she said. I began to caress her gently. At first she lay quiet, I thought she'd fallen asleep. Then she stirred under my fingers and said, 'Oh god I love you, oh god . . . Please make the world end!'

So we acted out our passion, and because we had travelled

so far from the world, it took us a little time to hear the banging on the gate, the shouts, the screaming.

I had barred the door. Gorvenal began hammering on it. 'Open up, Drustan, for Mithras' sake! The king's here.'

I saw Essylt's terrified eyes, just waking from ecstasy, felt her clinging arms still fast round my shoulders. I kissed her. 'Don't be frightened,' I said. My heart was beating wildly. I pulled my tunic over my head and unbarred the door.

As I did so I heard a grating cry, and Gorvenal fell inwards across the threshold. From his back protruded a long spear. One of the soldiers had run him through for trying to warn us. Branwen stood in the doorway of her room, staring across the hall, she held her baby in her arms. Her face was frozen with fear and Conn clung sobbing to her robe.

With his bodyguard around him, King Mark stood in the middle of the hall. Andret was jabbering at his elbow. 'See, lord, just as I told you. He never went away at all. Here's your proof!'

'Silence,' Mark said. He was staring at me. Behind me Essylt clutched the covers to her breast, silent. 'Oh Drustan,' Mark said slowly, 'oh Drustan . . . Why have you betrayed me?'

I knelt down, partly to get a good look at Gorvenal. There was nothing to be done, he was dead already. I closed his eyes. 'I'm sorry,' I said.

'*Sorry?*' Segward pushed forward, his voice cracking on a high note. 'Are you indeed? Well, you'll be a lot sorrier before tonight's ended, I can tell you that. Once you've had a taste of the hot irons and the pincers you'll know what contrition means. You'll wish you'd never even looked at the queen.'

'Enough,' said Mark wearily. 'He is a king's son and was once called my heir. He's not to be tortured. Let him be executed tomorrow with the axe.'

'At least let me die in a trial of strength!'

Mark smiled bitterly. 'Who can doubt that in any trial of strength you'd be the victor?' He turned to his soldiers. 'Take him back to Castle Dor, chain him and put him in the dungeon; but no torture, understand? And send a monk to be with him until it's time.'

'Let me get my clothes,' I said. This gave me a chance to look at Essylt and she at me. I didn't dare speak to her, but one look was enough. The world had ended for us, and in a way I knew she was glad.

Meanwhile Mark had taken Conn into his arms. Branwen knelt by Gorvenal's body, and as I passed her she raised her head and spat at me.

The soldiers seized my arms, and while they might have been forbidden the use of instruments of torture, I knew they'd make the most of whatever came to hand. I felt the leather thongs bite into my flesh and the blood run over my hands. They tried to force me out, but I threw myself down in front of Mark.

'Lord, at least tell me, what's to become of the queen?'

'Since you are to die,' he said, 'she need not. I shall find a suitable retreat for her, some abbey. I hope that if she does sufficiently stringent penance her soul may still be saved.'

'And your soul?' I asked.

He spoke so low that I could hardly hear. 'I loved you, Drustan, I made you my heir. I'm not god, my love has limits.' Then he said harshly, 'Take him away!'

They made me walk back to Castle Dor, tethered by an iron collar round my neck like a runaway slave. The going was very slow, and this gave me a chance to make a plan. The captain of the troop lashed me with his whip, sometimes he curled it round my ankles and made me fall over in the dark, but by the time we reached the cliffs it was quite light. They were intending to march me up the road beside the estuary while a messenger rode ahead to prepare the axeman and the people. This way they thought there was less chance of my escape.

Essylt had once told me that Samson, the Christian monk, had built an oratory on these cliffs. As the sky grew lighter I scanned the cliffs for its jagged outline, and I began to stumble, no hard part to act because I was exhausted. The captain swore at me.

'Wait, for god's sake!' I shouted. They drew rein and clustered round me in a circle.

'What is it now?' the captain asked.

'It's already dawn,' I said, 'and the king promised I should see a monk.'

'You'll be seeing god soon enough,' one of the soldiers said. 'What d'you want to see a monk for?' The others cackled with laughter.

'I'm a true Christian,' I said. 'I must tell my sins before I die.'

'First I've heard of it,' said one.

'What's a true Christian doing in bed with the queen?' asked another.

The captain, however, was baptised himself. 'You'll have to do without a monk,' he said, 'but Samson's oratory is hereabouts. I'll give you time to say a prayer there.'

We came to the oratory soon after.

It was built right on the cliff's edge of rough local stone stuck together with coarse clay. The doorway was not much higher than my head. The altar was at the opposite side from the door and above it a small window looked out over the sea.

'Let me go in alone,' I said.

They murmured among themselves. 'There's no way out but this,' I said, indicating the narrow door.

'Right,' said the captain, 'but you've an appointment to keep, remember?'

They all sniggered.

I went out and kneeled by the altar. A lamp was burning. Out of the corner of my eye I measured distances, angles. It might not be possible, but it was my only chance. With one leap I was on the altar, then I dived head first through the window. I felt the ground strike my chest, forcing the breath from my body, then I was skidding forwards, unable to stop myself, faster and faster. My hands and feet scrabbled for holds in the crumbling cliff edge, but found none. A tuft of dry grasses came out by the roots and I fell over the edge. I fell slowly, as if in a dream; I had time to notice the points of the rocks below, waiting to skewer my body.

# Twenty-Three

Someone was bathing my face. I turned my head and my mouth filled with brine . . . The sea. So I hadn't died! I tried to lift my head. Nothing happened. The next wave came and ebbed against my cheek. I could feel the wet sand under my body now, and the sharp lumps of stone. How long had I lain at the base of the cliff?

I tried again to raise my head. The sun was low. A big wave broke over my head. The tide was coming in, and if I couldn't move up the beach I'd drown.

I tried to move my arms and legs, and felt pain for the first time, sharp and terrible. Water filled my mouth, I choked. My whole body grew numb. I could hear the gulls screaming overhead, the splash of the eager, rising tide. The pain was worst in my chest, where I lay over a large sharp stone. My legs were on sand, I could wriggle my toes. My left arm was outflung over a large boulder, aching and useless.

I could see no soldiers, only a half moon of empty beach. I began to move, scrabbling with my knees and feet, striving to pull myself up over the rocks with my right hand. The rocks were shiny with seaweed, they must be covered at high tide. Did the tide reach right to the base of the cliffs?

I pillowed my cheek on a rock, panting with effort and let the sea wash over my head. I could see quite clearly below its depths the crabs and the little darting fish. Farther out the big fish waited. The sea would bloat my body like a pig; my hideous remains would be washed ashore on some beach to disgust the stolid fishermen.

I worked hard and got my head clear of the water.

165

The pain in my chest almost stopped me breathing, and I knew that my left arm was broken. It trailed tiredly behind. I gritted my teeth. There must be dry rock somewhere. I swore and heaved myself along, crawling, then collapsing on to me belly again like a half-crushed worm.

I thought I was finished when my grasping fingers found a handful of sand that didn't stick to them. It broke and ran away like flour: dry, and then a white rock: dry, not wetly green with seaweed.

I put my head down in the sand and cried. The sand stuck to my face like a golden crust.

My body was tenacious of life when by rights I should have died. I crawled into a cave in fear that Mark's soldiers might make a search for my body. Just before it grew dark I heard them calling to each other from the top of the cliffs, but they must have decided that the high tide had taken me, for my refuge wasn't discovered.

I don't know how long I lay there, without food or drink, racked by fever and a pain which prevented me from ever quite losing consciousness; but in one moment more lucid than the rest I realised that I mustn't lie in the cave any longer, because I'd starve to death.

So I emerged on hands and knees and began the slow lop-sided crawl across the beach, with my useless arm bumping painfully on the ground. My tongue had swollen and hung out of my mouth.

It took me all day, but I found a path and at last managed to drag myself to the top, after slipping to the bottom countless times. I lay at the top. A slow relaxation began to wash over me. Perhaps, I thought, I can rest here. *Essylt . . .* Essylt?

I saw a face quite close to mine and a mouth opening in a scream I didn't hear. A child stood over me, a skipping rope dangling, surrounded by a ring of fascinated children's faces . . . Blackness, then a thick-bearded man, then being lifted and blinding pain . . . Then nothing.

'Who *is* he, that's what I'd like to know.'
'Some sailor.'

166

'Can't he talk?'
'Don't seem so, though his tongue's all right. I 'ad a look.'
'He'd a collar round his neck.'
'A slave?'
'Looks so, but there's no brand. I made sure.'
Choking laughter. '. . . fine figure of a man!'

Lying on the floor in the fishermen's hut, while the women gossip and mend nets, the children play five stones with quick filthy fingers or poke me with sticks.

'Dun' 'e do nuthin'?'
'Nuthin'. Lie an' stare.'
'P'raps 'e be off 'is head,' tapping her forehead.
'Looks so.'
'Like a scarecrow, won't eat nuthin' beyon' a mouthful of broth.'
'A slave.'

Lying on the floor by a stinking pile of fish guts, watching the quick knives rip the silver flesh, the pale blood running down their thumbs. No knife to end my half-life, lighten my darkness, but how can I live through this? I must get away.

As soon as I could walk almost upright again I staggered off through the village. The villagers scattered before me, turning their heads away, as though I would bring evil on them. I lurched from their sight along the paths, the hedges just scattering their first spring flowers. I saw my shadow going before me in the morning, skulking along behind me in the afternoon. Sometimes I sang to keep it company.

> Tra la, tra lee, my love is true to me,
> And the oak and the ash and the fine thorn tree
> Bloom all about in my own country.

Sometimes as I sang my eyes couldn't help weeping, then I reproached myself, 'Come, Drustan, don't get faint-hearted. She'll never take you back, and then what will happen to the children?' Sometimes I said to myself, 'Look at the feet, they're bleeding, they've no boots. Look at the knees, cut to the bone by stones. The knees say they can't go on walking for ever without a rest. The thighs are lonely, the belly's empty, the genitals say, "Forget us, we don't exist. We repent all the wrong we did!" The heart's broken.' I had to answer myself too, as I had no companion, 'Hearts mend, don't let it delay you. Mark's waiting, Essylt will never forgive us. The children want their father to kiss them before they go to sleep. Sing a little, don't keep falling down.'

So I sang.

'Tra la, tra lee, my love is true to me.' I blundered off the road and fell into ditches and battled with brambles. When it was too dark to see I lay down and let my body rest, but my mind went on dancing.

Once, I don't know when or where, I blundered into a village. The bigger boys threw stones at me, the little ones howled. The men set their dogs on me, and I ran away. Another time I met a party of travellers with fine leather on their horses and big cloaks made of thick bright wool. They drew rein and barred my way.

'Who are you, fellow?' one asked me.

'Leave him be,' said his friend. 'Come away.'

'Better than you,' I said. 'An honest poet that the rain falls on.'

'You'd seem more honest if you weren't half naked,' the first one said.

'Come away!'

'Sing us a song then, you madman. Prove you're a poet.'

'I was schooled by the druids,' I said, 'and learned the art of magic. I lived with Myrddin the bard. Mourn for him; he died at Degannwy. I was heir to King Mark and swore faith with his queen. Why should I make music for rabble like you?'

'If you won't sing, at least you'll turn cartwheels.' He lashed my legs with his riding whip so I jumped in the air. They all laughed.

Their laughter echoed with pain down my dreams.

168

Then one night the moon smiled at me.

I walked upright through high gates and heard the chant:

'*Lauda anima mea Dominum, laudabo Dominum vita mea: psallam Domino meo quamdiu fuero . . .*'

I was laid on a bed and gentle hands washed me. I was given broth. Then I saw her face. Reed thin, pale as moonlight. Was it a dream? All my pain, all my madness, at the sight of her, vanished like a breath of wind.

# Twenty-Four

'Essylt!' I said.

'Hush.'

'Essylt, don't you know me?'

'I knew you from the first. Don't speak. They mustn't know.'

'This is fate . . . that I should come to the very place where you were sent . . .'

'It is fate,' she said.

While I was still sick I could do nothing to help her. As a penance she had the most menial work of all, washing bandages, emptying slops. And she, who had been used to a soft bed with fur covers, and the choicest food, slept on the ground, ate dry bread and drank water.

My bones mended and slowly my strength returned. I could watch her about her work; and I loved her then more than I had ever loved her in the days when she was a queen.

We made a plan. When spring came we would escape together and go into hiding in the great Moresk forest. I would hunt for her and make her a house of leaves. We did not speak about the winter, for we both knew how it would end, but it seemed enough that we should have one summer together, and when I found myself alone once more I resolved that I would go hunting the wild boar again.

I roused her from sleep one moonless night in early spring, and hand in hand we crept between the low, mean buildings of the nunnery. I lifted her over the wall, and we set off together towards the forest. We had one bundle between us, but the sword I had managed to steal hung comfortingly from the leather belt round my waist. Before we had gone far I was carrying her. I found that my strength had returned almost completely. I was slower than before and leaner, but my powers of endurance were greater now. I carried her in my arms with her head resting on my shoulder, her eyes closed, the bundle strapped to my back.

I didn't feel safe till we had reached the outskirts of the forest, and the great trees hid us from the world outside, then I made us a bed on the ground, and undressed her.

Beneath her tunic was a small bodice of rough skin, and when I took that off, I saw that, from shoulder to waist, her back and all her beautiful breast was rubbed raw by friction from the coarse hair.

I couldn't speak at first. 'Who —?'

'Oh, all of them. I couldn't refuse . . . One gets used to it.'

I took the thing away and buried it beneath a rotting tree.

The nuns had also cropped her hair close to her head. She looked like a child. I knelt at her feet. 'Essylt —'

'I wish you need not see me like this. I wish I could hide from you until my hair has grown and my skin is healed.'

'You don't understand. Have I loved you all this while for nothing?'

We lay down, and I placed the sword between us.

'That is for Mark,' I said, 'a sacrifice for his honour. Until your flesh is sound I will put the sword between us.'

We wandered in the depths of the forest restless and in haste, like beasts that are hunted. We hardly ever dared return at night to last night's shelter. We ate only the flesh of wild animals, partially cooked over smoking fires, and such roots and berries as we could find. We drank spring water. Time lost its meaning. Our clothes grew ragged, for the briars tore them, but we loved each other, and this was happiness.

Summer was ending, and one day by chance we came upon a small clearing. In it was a single hut, built of interlaced branches and daubed with mud. In front of this hut an old hermit was praying on his knees. It was too late to turn back. He opened his eyes and saw us. 'Say nothing,' I whispered to Essylt.

'God bless you,' the hermit called out in a voice that sounded cracked like an old bell, and rusty from little use. 'Are you lost? Shall I direct you to the ouskirts of the forest? I know a path that will take you near Castle Dor.'

'We aren't lost,' I said, 'though I thank you for your advice. We won't disturb you any longer at your prayers.'

'No, no wait,' the hermit said. 'This is very strange. I am Ogrin, I've lived here in the forest for longer than I can remember, but you're the first living souls I've seen who haven't been hunting or lost. Tell me, who you are?'

He gave us water from a muddy bowl and a handful of blackberries. We sat on the ground.

'I am Kai,' I said, 'this is my sister Eithne. The call came to us to renounce the world, so we wander in this forest. My sister is dumb. Angels point the way to her.'

The hermit had long filthy hair, but beneath his matted locks his eyes were shrewd. 'Why do you wear a sword?'

'So god's will directs me,' I said. 'Please say a prayer for us before we go on our way.'

He prayed. 'The end of the world is coming, O god. Save your faithful servants who have left the world of men with its vanities and lust. Keep us pure and strong against temptations as you kept Saint Anthony. Grant us your peace.'

I took Essylt's hand and was about to leave him, but he came over to us and took her face between his hands. 'You see angels, my child?' She nodded. 'I too, once, long ago . . .' He made the sign of the cross on her forehead. 'Bless you, you have a gift more precious than speech.' He seemed not to see that she had begun to weep.

'Goodbye,' I said, leading her away.

'God bless you too, my son,' he said.

Winter came. We lived hidden in the hollow of a rock and on the frozen earth the cold crisped our bed with dead leaves. I was lucky enough to waylay two farm lads on their way through the forest and stole all their clothes and gear. Essylt dressed in the thick tunic of the younger boy. Her skin had healed and we slept in each other's arms, forgetting our cold and hunger.

'How old will Conn be now?' she asked me once.

'Five,' I said, 'or six.'

'Is it so long?' she said.

Spring returned again, and we would sometimes hear the sounds of the hunt, dogs baying and the rush of a frightened creature through the undergrowth, but we stayed away from the wild boars' lairs and so kept ourselves out of double danger. But the world reached for us, all the same.

We were lying by the banks of a stream, watching the flies dancing on the surface of the water. The grass was bright with cowslips, and a kingfisher with shimmering wings swooped low over the stream. Suddenly Essylt sat up and clutched my arm. 'What's that?'

We heard a strange rustling in the bushes, a dragging and thumping.

Essylt dived for her tunic and put it on. We often went naked when the sun was warm, both for the pleasure of it and to save our clothes. Her hair had grown out in tangled curls to her shoulders. She was as thin as a needle and very brown.

'It's the hermit,' she said.

Ogrin emerged on to the bank and stood blinking in the sunlight. He was panting and leaning heavily on a rough wooden crutch.

'I've been searching for you,' he said, 'searching the paths and trackways since Easter time: for now I know who you are.' He turned to Essylt. 'Lady, you're no more dumb than I am, are you?'

She said softly, 'No, father, I'm not.'

Then he turned to me. 'Lord Drustan, I am here to tell you of the oath that the lords of Kernow have taken. King Mark has promised this – whoever can capture you will be richly rewarded both with lands and gold. All the nobles have sworn to find you, alive or dead. I've come to call you to penance, Drustan. God pardons sinners who turn to repentance.'

I felt Essylt's hand grow cold in mine, and was filled with fury. I longed to tumble Ogrin into the stream and hold him down until he could no longer struggle.

'Of what are you asking me to repent, Ogrin?' I said. 'You sit in judgement over us, do you? Do you know what cup it was we drank on the high seas? We are drunk with it still. I would rather beg all my life or live on roots and herbs with Essylt than be king of a wide kingdom without her.'

The hermit said, 'God aid you, lord Drustan, you've lost both this world and the next. A man who turns traitor to his king deserves to be torn apart by horses and burned. Wherever his ashes fall no grass will grow. The land will be barren, the trees and green things will die. You must give back this woman to King Mark. He is your uncle, and her rightful husband according to god's law.'

'He put her away and sent her to the nuns,' I said. 'She was no longer his wife or a queen, only a drudge. I rescued her. I've hunted and killed for her and guarded her all the time we've been together in this forest. She belongs to me now.'

Ogrin sat down. Essylt knelt in front of him, her head on his knees, and wept quietly. 'Unhappy lady,' he said, 'I must remind you of the wise saying of one of the fathers of the church. "Do you not know that you are Eve? You are the devil's doorway. It was you who profaned the Tree of Life, and you who beguiled man into sin . . ." ' He recited psalms to her and said many prayers, but she went on weeping, and shook her head.

'It grieves me,' Ogrin said, 'but what comfort can one offer the dead? Do penance, Drustan, for a man or woman who lives in sin without repenting is quite dead.'

'Oh, no,' I said, 'I'm alive. I do no penance, it's an evil thing. We'll go back into the forest, that's our home now . . . Essylt, will you come?'

She left him without a word and came to me, I put my arm round her shoulders and we went back into the wood.

The trees hid us with their branches. The tapestry of leaves fell behind us.

We went into hiding. I no longer dared leave her to hunt, so that food was scarce, and the first frost filled my heart with dread. I built a stout shelter for our last resting place, and she lay beneath the canopy of leaves and we talked whole days away, and I sang her songs. Sometimes she fancied she was at Dun Ailinne, a virgin in her father's house, and I had come to woo her; sometimes that we were on the ship bound for Castle Dor. I played these games to please her.

But the child I'd got on her that summer took all her strength, and one night there was blood. The child bled away from her and she wept. 'Oh Drustan, I wanted so much to give you another son.'

'You will,' I said. 'You will when you are strong.'

I knew she was dying: of hunger and cold. She needed warmth, rich food, wine; everything that waited at Castle Dor. Mark could give her life, if he would.

Her thin hand in mine, I thought of the girl, my mother, that I had killed. I thought of Cerridwen, of Cunaide, of Gorvenal, of Myrddin, all those that my love had destroyed. And I knew that Essylt must not die.

I carried her out of the forest, to the clearing where Ogrin's hut stood. I made a canopy from the branches of trees and laid her beneath it. Then I fetched the hermit.

'Here is the queen,' I said. 'You are my witness. I am giving her back to King Mark. She's very sick. They must look after her well, and then she will recover.'

'But, lord,' said Ogrin, 'how can the king take her back? You and she have lived in sin together this past year, and more.'

'There has been no sin,' I said. 'Let me swear you an oath.'

He said, 'Swear then.'

'As I hope for eternal life, I swear that there was never any sin between the queen and me; not while we have lived together in the forest, nor before at Castle Dor, nor ever.

If we lay in one bed my sword was always between us. The queen has been cruelly wronged. If I am lying may I burn in hell for ever.'

'That is a powerful oath,' said Ogrin.

'Let him come for her,' I said.

'You have my word.'

I went back to the bower where Essylt lay. On her hand was the ring I had sent her, but her fingers were so wasted that it hardly held. No wind blew and no leaves stirred, but through a crevice in the branches a sunbeam fell on Essylt's face, and it shone white like ice.

I kissed her lips. She sighed and half woke.

'I must leave you, love, for a little while,' I said. 'If you need me, send and I will come. If I ever send for you, you must promise to come to me.'

'Drustan?' she murmured. Her eyes closed again.

I left her. I gave her back to life.

# Twenty-Five

'And that was the end. I have told you all. I have told you from the beginning, as you asked . . . But there is no more.'

My wife sat still, her brown hair falling over her breasts, her hands clasped below her pregnant belly.

'Drustan, it's twenty years from that day. You have wandered the earth, from Africa to Ynys Orc. You are married to me, and I have borne you sons and daughters . . . How can you say that was the end?'

I moved restlessly on the bed. 'I didn't want my life . . There are kinds of love that cannot be broken, chains that will fetter my soul to hers for ever.'

'It seems as though I always knew,' she said. 'It was like a story I'd heard before. So much suffering . . . It was *cruel* of you to marry me.'

'I was weary of wandering,' I said. 'Weary of being alone.'

'I've loved you.'

'I've been alone.'

'Couldn't you find it in your heart to pity me?'

'Pity? No, why? You were only a shadow. Essylt of Armorica . . . The other Essylt . . .'

She stood up, heavy and awkward, and leaned on the parapet that looked out over the sea. The wind blew back the hair from her face. 'I have loved you,' she said through her tears, 'in my way as well as she. *Why* couldn't you forget her?'

'I'm thirsty,' I said. 'Give me some water.'

She poured water from a stone jug and handed me the cup. I pulled myself up on the narrow bed. Knowing that I would never recover from this wound, I had had myself brought here, to the top room of the watchtower which overlooked the harbour. Here I could lie and gaze at the sea, waiting for the ship that would bring my love to me for the last time.

For she would come.

I had sent spies regularly back and forth to Castle Dor. My love still lived. King Mark had grown old, loving her as devotedly as ever. And my son Conn had grown into a fine young man, a mighty warrior, ruler of all Kernow when Mark dies.

'Can you see the ship?'

'There is no ship,' she said.

'The ship will come,' I said. 'Its sails will be white. Essylt has my message and she will come.'

My wife rubbed her back. 'You are sick with the past. How do you know she hasn't forgotten you long ago?'

Pain clouded my thoughts and I no longer knew truth from unreality. We must be together, I thought, because we share the same soul; we drank the golden wine. We have no choice. But what if this is darkness and illusion. Will I be alone for ever?

I cannot believe so.

Last night I had a dream.

A man lay dying. His face was turned towards the sea. He was waiting for a ship. He turned and looked at me, and I saw that the man was myself.

He was waiting for the ship that was bringing Essylt from Kernow to keep her promise to come to him before he died, but the ship was too long in coming, and he was alone. He asked, 'How long must I be patient?'

Slowly a ship with white sails glided into the harbour. Tears ran down the cheeks of the dying man. 'I should have gone to her,' he said. 'I have been apart from my soul too long.'

Time passed, and his breathing was hard, but he was content to wait. Only a little while now, he thought, and we will be together.